Southwesterly

Wind

Also by Luiz Alfredo Garcia-Roza

The Silence of the Rain
December Heat
A Window in Copacabana

A NOVEL

Southwesterly
Wind

Luiz Alfredo

GARCIA-ROZA

translated by Benjamin Moser

PICADOR
HENRY HOLT AND COMPANY
NEW YORK

www.picadorusa.com

Picador® is a U.S. registered trademark and is used by Henry Holt and Company under license from Pan Books Limited.

For information on Picador Reading Group Guides, as well as ordering, please contact the Trade Marketing department at St. Martin's Press.
Phone: 1-800-221-7945 extension 763
Fax: 212-677-7456
E-mail: trademarketing@stmartins.com

Library of Congress Cataloging-in-Publication Data

Garcia-Roza, L. A. (Luiz Alfredo)
    [Vento sudoeste. English]
    Southwesterly wind / Luiz Alfredo Garcia-Roza ; translated by Benjamin Moser.
        p. cm.
    ISBN 0-312-42454-X
    EAN 978-0312-42454-1
    I. Title.
  PQ9698.17.A745
  869.3'42—dc21   2003056638

First published in Brazil under the title *Vento sudoeste* by Companhia das Letras, São Paulo

First published in the United States by Henry Holt and Company

First Picador Edition: January 2005

10 9 8 7 6 5 4 3 2 1

Southwesterly
Wind

At four in the afternoon, the little neighborhood restaurant was empty. The only waiter, toward the back, divided his attention between a pile of plates in front of him and the television perched in the corner of the room. Eyes glued to the screen, he took a plate, sprayed some alcohol on it, wiped it off, and stacked it on another pile next to the first one. He did it unhurriedly, at the pace of the TV movie. Once he was done, he separated the plates into two perfectly equal piles; the movement forced him to tear his eyes away from the screen. Then he moved on to the silverware. He took the pieces out of a plastic box to his left, sprayed them with the cleaner, and, after carefully wiping them, tossed them into another box to his right. This task was harder to coordinate with the TV because the box was divided into compartments for spoons, forks, and knives, and it was almost impossible to select the right compartment without looking.

The repetitive, monotonous sound of the silverware being tossed into the box added to Espinosa's irritation, and made it harder for him to concentrate on the conversation.

"I don't do odd jobs."

"I know you don't, Sergeant."

"But that's what you're proposing."

"I need help."

"Why don't you hire a private investigator?"

"I don't know any. I know they exist; I see their ads in the papers—they seem more interested in catching people cheating on their wives."

"And what do you want me to investigate?"

"A murder."

"A murder?"

"Right."

"Who got killed?"

"I don't know yet."

"You don't know him?"

"No, he's not dead yet."

"Not dead yet?"

"Well, there's no body. Nobody's been killed . . . yet."

With every passing minute, Espinosa regretted more deeply that he had agreed to this meeting.

"You've been bugging me for a week about *this*? You want me to investigate the murder of someone—you don't know who—who isn't even dead? Are you screwing around with me?"

"No, Sergeant. Please, I know it looks weird . . ."

"It *looks* weird?"

"Sorry."

"And can you tell me where, and why, this murder is going to take place?"

"N . . . No . . . I'm so sorry."

"And naturally you don't know who the murderer is going to be."

"I do."

"Sorry?"

"Me."

"You're planning on committing murder?"

"Not if you put it so . . . clearly."

"Clearly? Son, the only thing missing in all this talk is clarity."

"You're right, sir. Maybe I should explain, even though it's not all that clear even to me."

"If it's not too much trouble, of course."

"I understand your irritation, Sergeant."

"So please get to the point."

"A psychic saw that I would commit a murder before my next birthday. There's less than two months to go."

"A psychic?"

"I mean, not one of the ones who wear turbans . . ."

"I know."

"Last year, some friends from work were with me in a bar celebrating my birthday. One of the people there, who wasn't with us, offered to give me a birthday present: a reading of my future. I'm completely skeptical about that kind of thing, but it seemed like fun and my friends kept at me, so I agreed. The guy made a few general predictions, the kind all psychics make, and then finished by saying that before my next birthday I would kill somebody and that the murder wouldn't be an accident."

"And you believed him?"

"I had to. He didn't have any reason to be telling me something like that."

"And how long before your next birthday?"

"Less than two months."

"And you want me to find out whom you're going to kill?"

"Yes, sir, if you will. I can't pay very much."

The kid spoke calmly. His diction was clear, and Espinosa could see in his eyes that he'd been suffering for a long time.

Espinosa recovered his usual tone: calm, deliberate, devoid of irony or irritation.

"Our meeting began badly. My fault. Let's go to the station, and we can resume our conversation there. It won't be anything official, unless you want it to be." He stood up, left some money on the table in exchange for the nothing they had consumed, and invited the kid to follow him with a friendly gesture.

It was winter, which meant, in Rio de Janeiro, that the days were pretty, the sky blue, and the temperature pleasant. The light was softer, shadows less sharply defined, and the colors less vibrant than in summer. It wasn't more than a ten-minute walk to the station. Espinosa figured the kid couldn't have been more than thirty. Medium height, pleasant face, dark hair. Like Espinosa, when he talked he looked his companion in the eyes, which made even small talk seem intense. When they arrived, he paused in front of the arch that covered the entrance to the building.

"You don't have to say anything against your will; if we don't make an official record of our conversation, it won't be anything more than a conversation."

Despite his deep voice, Espinosa spoke softly. He didn't have to talk the guy into coming in. The old three-story building on the Rua Hilário de Gouveia, in the middle of Copacabana, was only two blocks from the beach. The entrance was always open, but the windows on the facade were always closed, to shut out the noise outside. Despite its age and function, the building was in a reasonable state of repair.

From the way the kid looked around, it was clear that everything in there was new to him. He seemed a little more comfortable in Espinosa's office.

"When you first called you said your name was Gabriel."

"That's right."

"Why do you believe in the psychic's prediction?"

"Because he'd never seen me before and he didn't have any motive for making such an accusation. And the way he said it didn't leave any reasonable doubt. At least not for me. I was terrified. To say that I took it seriously is an understatement. I panicked. My friends thought it was a riot."

"So what do you think?"

"I don't think anyone should play soccer unless they have some talent for the sport."

"That's not exactly what I wanted to find out."

"Sorry. What did you want to find out, sir?"

"If you want to kill anyone."

"Nobody . . . in particular."

"And in general?"

"In general?"

"Yes."

"In general . . ."

~~~

The leftover material from the curtains was just enough to make a cushion for the windowsill. The fact that it was on the ground floor was her favorite feature of the apartment. The window facing the street was high enough to protect her from indiscreet glances, and just large enough for Dona Alzira to use it as a perch. At the end of the afternoon, she sat there waiting for her son to turn the corner from the Rua do Catete onto the Rua Buarque de Macedo. Gabriel had his father's pleasant face and strong body, but he was much more intelligent. She'd never seen *him* drunk or heard about *him* getting involved with hookers. He'd had the same job ever since he had gotten his degree in business administration, and thanks to him they'd gotten a mortgage on the apartment. The two-bedroom flat was dark, and despite her daily efforts to keep it clean, it was insistently invaded by roaches from the trash cans in the central patio. Nothing helped; every morning when she got up to make her son's breakfast, Dona Alzira found, on the floor of the kitchen or even the living room, one or two of those disgusting insects lying on its back, still moving its legs.

None of this affected in the least her joy in living with her son and taking care of him. Since she was short, she had ordered a little wooden stepstool so that she could easily climb up onto the windowsill. Her eyes weren't good enough for her to see all the way to the corner; she could make out the movement of the cars on the Rua do Catete but she couldn't distinguish them clearly. As for the pedestrians, she couldn't even tell if they were men or women. So she couldn't exactly see her son turning the corner, but amid the crowds of people who were constantly turning onto Buarque de Macedo, she always knew beyond a shadow of a doubt which one was her Gabriel. She could identify him long before she could actually see him—from his size, from the way he walked—until he finally came into focus. It felt like her own life was taking shape.

On that afternoon, at the appointed hour, she took up her post, already savoring the pleasure of seeing him turn the corner. After fifteen minutes, a slight uneasiness came over her, starting at her neck. After another fifteen minutes the uneasiness became pain. She came down the ladder, checked to see that the phone wasn't off the hook (he never failed to call when he was running late), that it was plugged in, that she hadn't misread the clock. When, almost forty minutes late, after she'd confused him with countless men, she saw her son emerge from the crowd, she had almost passed out. Her worries didn't seem to be unfounded; Gabriel was walking more slowly than usual. His shoulders were slumped, and he was looking at the ground. What she was seeing was more than mere fatigue. She made the sign of the cross.

As soon as she heard the key slide into the door, she pulled herself together; she didn't want her son to see that she'd been upset.

"Gabriel, honey, did you have to stay late at work?"

"No, Mother."

"There must have been a problem with the subway because of the new line they're building, right?"

"No, Mother, there was no problem with the subway."

"All right . . . I don't want to nag."

She mutely scanned her son's face, trying to decipher the minuscule signs that were, to her terror, growing less intelligible with each passing day. She couldn't have said exactly when it had started, what she called her son's area of darkness. Up until then, she had thought of him as made up of pure light, clear and transparent as crystal. Last year, she'd started noticing the first shadows; and that evening, when he turned the corner, her son had seemed frighteningly opaque.

"Mom, I already told you not to worry if I'm late; things happen . . ."

"What happened?"

"Nothing happened, Mother. Everything's fine."

"If you have to say that everything's fine, that means something's wrong."

"Mother . . ."

"I know something's bothering you. I'm sure of it. Is it a woman?"

"Mother . . ."

"Sorry. I don't have any business meddling in your life."

"Mom, of course you do. You always have. I just don't want you getting all worried for no reason."

The furniture in the living room was heavy and dark.

The chairs were covered with purple velvet. There was a *Last Supper* and two scenes of the countryside at dusk. It wasn't a very cozy room. They rarely used it; it was really no more than a passageway from the kitchen to the bedrooms. The constant foot traffic had forced Dona Alzira to cover the rug with transparent plastic, in order to ensure that the floral motif remained visible. While they were talking, she touched her son's shirtsleeve. They seldom touched each other's skin; even their hands rarely made contact. Gabriel bypassed his mother, lightly touching the shawl on her shoulder, and went into his room, closing the door. She interpreted the gesture as clear evidence that something was wrong, though when he came home he always went into his room and closed the door. Even with the door closed, Dona Alzira "saw" her son take off his work clothes, put on the shorts she'd given him for Christmas, plug in his earphones, and lie down to listen to classical music. At least it wasn't disco.

While she was fixing up the little table in the kitchen for dinner, she thought again about whether she should talk to Father Crisóstomo about her son. Ever since her husband had died, when Gabriel was nine, she'd taken Father Crisóstomo as her confessor and family counselor. He would know, just as he always did, what was happening with her Gabriel and what to do about it. But she was afraid that direct intervention from a third party could threaten the relationship she had with her son. She couldn't stand to see her boy leave home; if she had to lose him, she'd rather it be by death, hers or his. God forgive her such feelings, but they were exactly what she thought; she would risk eternal damnation in order not to lose her son while she had breath in her body. They ate dinner in silence.

He wasn't sure he'd made the best decision. At first, the sergeant had seemed irritated, unhappy to have agreed to meet with him; suddenly, without warning, he had apologized and become understanding and sensitive. Which aspect of the officer's personality should he trust? Both? The first was so disagreeable that it had irremediably polluted the second. Now he wondered if he'd done the right thing by going to the police. He thought that cops were like priests: even if you haven't done anything, they think you're guilty. He took off his earphones in order to concentrate better as he reviewed every moment of the conversation. He wasn't so much worried about the cop's words. It was the tone, his mood he was trying to reconstruct. The initial moments, hostile and punctuated with irony, didn't count as a real conversation. He didn't remember what he had said to make the cop's attitude change, or what had happened to make him invite him back to the precinct. At any rate, the second part of the conversation was indisputably better than the first. There was still something he didn't quite get, though. The sergeant didn't promise to investigate; he hadn't even bothered to take down his name, address, telephone number, things like that, and yet he seemed sympathetic to Gabriel's problems. In fact,

Gabriel felt like someone who goes to the doctor because he's suffering from some deep affliction and leaves the doctor's office without a prescription, only the doctor's kind words.

He replaced the earphones and stretched out on the bed. His room was a lot smaller than his mother's, but he used every inch of the space. There wasn't a single empty space on his wall, which was entirely taken up, hidden by his wardrobe, shelves for books and CDs, his desk; even his bed was up against the wall, in a kind of niche between the shelves. He didn't have enough room to move around in; he couldn't take two steps, and if he stood in the middle of the room and stretched out his arms, he would bump into something. That was one of the reasons he took walks at night, which inevitably made his mother upset and suspicious. The room was a perfect expression of himself: functional, but without any free space.

The sergeant had been unmoved by the offer of payment. In fact, he'd seemed irritated by the suggestion. That was the moment when the meeting had started going downhill, and if Gabriel hadn't been so determined to stick to the subject, the meeting would have been a complete disaster—though he suspected it had been a disaster anyway. What kind of investigation could be done if the investigator doesn't even bother to write down the name of the person he's investigating, much less his address or his place of employment? Did he think Gabriel was crazy, and decide not to confront him? Maybe inviting him back to the station had been a way of shrugging him off more easily. That possibility was the worst, because it automatically voided everything the man had said. Gabriel would have to talk to him again to find out if that was true.

In spite of the earphones, he could still hear the banging on the door. He got up, annoyed by the interruption, opened the door, and came face-to-face with his mother, who was brandishing a tray.

"Coffee. I just made it."

Without a word, Gabriel took the cup, placed it on his table, and turned back to close the door. He didn't like being disturbed in his refuge, but he was moved by his mother's small kindnesses. It was her way of apologizing for needling him. But if he showed her that he was touched, she might set up a full bar at his door.

He focused anew on his conversation with the sergeant. He remembered that the man's change in attitude had taken place when Gabriel had answered his question about whether he believed in the psychic's prediction. Strange, that the cop was more interested in a personal opinion than in any concrete facts. He hadn't actually provided him with any concrete facts. He'd only spoken of his intuitions, which is why the officer might have written him off as one of those lunatics who hang around police stations complaining about imaginary persecutors.

The difference between the lunatics and Gabriel was that Gabriel knew that what was threatening him wasn't imaginary; he wasn't confusing reality and fantasies—he knew exactly what was real and what was not. His feeling about the oracle was real, and that was why he sought out the sergeant: not for an objective fact, but for a subjective yet concrete impression. He wasn't crazy—he was sure of that. At least, he wasn't any crazier than anybody else. He had some problems, that was true, but nothing that made him crazier than normal. His relationship with his mother was one of those difficulties, but he was pretty sure he could straighten that one out soon enough.

When he looked at the coffee, he noticed that it had gone cold. If he gave it back to his mother untouched, she would take that as a slap in the face, and he didn't want to add anything else to the slightly hostile climate created by his late arrival. He was twenty-nine; he shouldn't have to make excuses to his mother for being a few minutes late. But then again, it wasn't all her fault. If he hadn't always been so punctual she wouldn't have gotten used to waiting for him at the window every afternoon. And in any case, he was the one who had led her to expect a phone call whenever he was running late. He couldn't just take away the security he'd given her. He opened his bedroom door, trying not to make noise, went to the bathroom, dumped the coffee into the toilet, and flushed. Before he could close his door again, he heard his mother's voice from the neighboring room:

"The coffee wasn't good, son?"

⋙

Espinosa lived only a few blocks from the station, which allowed him to walk to work. He took different routes: one, more direct, if he was in a hurry; others, if there was something he wanted to check out along the way. Tonight he left the station later than usual—he'd had to make up for the time he'd spent with the guy. It was already dark when he passed the reception desk on the ground floor and said good night to the people on the night shift. The heavy traffic on the Rua Barata Ribeiro, only a few feet away, made no impression on him; it was just the audiovisual background to his thoughts.

He started walking home without paying attention to what was going on around him, automatically weaving his way through the people approaching from the opposite direction. Moments like this were taken up by intense mental activity; his body worked like an automaton. Shoulders stooped, hands in pockets, he kept his eyes on the ground. He thought of himself as intelligent, but not brainy. His fantasies were just as important to him, if not more important, than his thoughts, and the two frequently got confused. His rational thoughts were often transformed into a series of flickering images.

He was most impressed by the guy's character: both absurd and truthful. To ask the police to investigate a murder that he himself would commit at some unknown date—a murder of an unknown victim—was completely absurd. And that was precisely what made the story ring true. Nobody would do something like that otherwise, unless they were crazy or acting in bad faith. And the boy's anguish seemed real enough. Espinosa had decided not to do anything, in case the kid wanted to keep the case private. He was a police sergeant, not a private investigator. Besides, how could he justify an investigation based on a pure fantasy, without a single fact to its name?

Espinosa had managed to transfer one of his old colleagues to his precinct. His colleague had been seriously wounded during an investigation they had jointly conducted, and now he was back on duty. The doctors had suggested that he refrain from violent encounters for a while. Welber was a cop Espinosa believed in completely. Maybe Gabriel's case would be a way for Welber to ease himself back into the service. But for that, there would have to be a case, and he wasn't at all convinced there was.

He turned left onto the Rua Anita Garibaldi, heading toward the Peixoto District, where he lived. Even though it was called a district, it was in truth only a small neighborhood, a few blocks of low-rise buildings around a central square, right in the middle of Copacabana. It would be a nice way to put his friend back to work. If Welber hadn't headed toward the door to intercept the kidnapper, Espinosa himself would have taken the bullet that almost cost his friend his life. He stopped to buy some beer and smoked ham, to give himself another option for dinner. He wasn't sure why he believed the kid. Even if he did believe him, that didn't mean that anything was going to happen, or that the psychic's prediction was going to come true. He'd never heard of a birthday-party clairvoyant making a prediction that came to pass, except when they said things like "You will travel abroad" or "You will soon meet the woman of your life." A trip abroad was an old psychic standard; and Espinosa thought that every woman in one's life could turn out to be the woman of one's life. It was true, however, that he'd never heard of a spiritualist making a prediction involving murder. Especially at a party. It must have been some pervert who hated birthdays. One advantage of giving the case to Welber was that he and Gabriel were the same age, which would facilitate communication between them. That is, if the detective felt like taking the story seriously.

At that hour, the square was practically deserted. Espinosa kept walking down the sidewalk, avoiding the earthen pathways through the square. He crossed the street that surrounded the square and entered the three-story building where he'd lived since he was ten years old, when his parents were still alive. He went to the top floor. He'd speak to Welber the next day. It wasn't exactly a case, but it was an opportunity for Welber to familiarize himself with the kind of people who show up at the Twelfth Precinct. He went up the two flights of stairs carrying the beer bottles, the ham, and a loaf of bread. There were still enough TV dinners in the freezer, but there wasn't enough variety: tagliatelle Bolognese, spaghetti Bolognese, or lasagna Bolognese. Everything else had already been eaten.

He had always been fond of the French window in the living room, which opened onto a little balcony with a cast-iron railing. The Venetian blinds, which extended from the floor almost to the ceiling, were a holdover from days when buildings were built to be pleasant to live in. He left his shopping bag in the kitchen, opened the blinds, closed the windows to keep out the cold, turned on a lamp, and sat softly on the sofa. Since leaving the station he'd tried not to move too abruptly, as if that would help keep his ideas from bumping into one another.

He wasn't entirely sure why he'd agreed to meet with the guy, and he was even less sure why he'd already given the case semiofficial status. It didn't do any good to sit on the sofa, staring at buildings and contemplating the landscape. A series of tasks, like taking a shower, making sandwiches for dinner, sorting his clothes for the wash, would divert his attention from the story for a while.

An hour later, though, his mind was still on the same questions; of the jobs he had laid out for himself, the only thing he'd done was take a shower. Then he remembered he hadn't put the beer in the refrigerator. He got dressed and went out to eat somewhere with better service.

Gabriel knew that his mother wouldn't listen in on his phone calls while the evening soap was on. And he knew that Olga would be home because she'd left work early, claiming to have the flu. Maybe she was sick and already asleep. He dialed, paying close attention to make sure his mother wasn't lifting her phone off the hook. There was no click on the line, and Olga herself answered.

"Gabriel . . . what a surprise . . ."

"How are you doing?"

"I've got a little fever and my body aches, but I think I'll be able to make it in to work tomorrow. Thanks for calling."

"Olga?"

"Yes?"

"I hope you feel better . . ."

"Gabriel."

"Huh."

"Is there something you want to tell me?"

"No . . . nothing. . . . Get well."

"Thanks."

Olga had witnessed the scene with the clairvoyant. She had arrived at the bar with another coworker just as the psychic was being introduced to the group. At the time, she'd thought his prediction was extremely aggressive and in astonishingly bad taste; she'd decided the guy was drunk. Before she'd said her good-byes, she'd noticed how upset Gabriel was and tried to dismiss the whole thing. That was the only time they'd ever mentioned the subject. And it was precisely the excessive emphasis she'd placed on the incident that had intensified Gabriel's concern. Exorcisms, like demons, are excessive, he thought.

Olga's testimony might help convince the sergeant that the story was true, but Gabriel couldn't picture Olga at the police station. She was as fragile as a tightrope walker. Not physically—her body was strong and healthy, her current cold notwithstanding—but emotionally she seemed on the verge of slipping. Judging from her caution around other people, a fall would no doubt be fatal. A meeting between

Olga and Espinosa would only be possible outside a police setting.

The birthday party had been the only time they'd met outside the office, and he thought she hadn't gone for him, but for another colleague. Even at work, he didn't see her as often as he'd like; they worked in different departments—he was technical, she was administrative. Olga had joined the company more than a year before, and they hadn't spoken often enough to have developed a real friendship. This was the first time he'd ever called her.

"Did you need to talk to someone, son?" His mother's voice, coming from her room and confused with the sound of the television, caught him as he was entering the bathroom.

"Nothing important, Mom, except that I'm going to kill someone."

"What, sweetheart?"

"Nothing, Mother."

Nobody at the party had paid any attention to the psychic's words. At least, nobody had brought up the subject later. They seemed to write it off as nothing more than simple bad taste. He saw it differently, though. It wasn't a question of the truth or falsity of the statement. What mattered was its effect. After the initial impact, the idea had slowly taken hold. Now, with only a little less than two months to go before his birthday, his body and soul were completely dominated. He went to sleep thinking about the seer's sentence, and it was the first thing that came to him when he awoke. In the last few months, he hadn't had a single conversation that wasn't affected by the idea; he hadn't had a single thought that wasn't corrupted by it; he hadn't had a single feeling that wasn't polluted by it. He wasn't afraid of going crazy: for all he knew, he already was crazy. He was afraid of succumbing to exhaustion. His mother had certainly already noticed that something extraordinary was going on, but she would never be able to guess exactly what. She probably suspected that he was madly in love with someone, and that would lead her to redouble her pleas to the Lord to put her son back on the right path. At night his fantasies became even more menacing, but he went to sleep, thankful that at least his dreams were still immune.

Even though Olga hadn't completely recovered from her cold, she headed back to work with a new curiosity: what had Gabriel meant by his phone call? His voice had sounded like someone asking for comfort, not offering it; he, not she, was the sick one. The subway train was full that morning, which didn't help her physical state. She couldn't find a seat, and she had worn too many layers to protect herself against the very slight chill in the air. She lived in Tijuca, and working in Copacabana meant she had a long commute. A few times, she and Gabriel had run into each other on the train; he got on at Catete. It was rare, but when it happened she noticed that he seemed to be pleased to see her. At the Uruguaiana station, downtown, the trains spit passengers out like an assembly line expelling finished products. Olga found a seat next to the window. When the train stopped at Catete, she scanned the platform; no sign of Gabriel. During the trip to Copacabana, she couldn't stop thinking about the curse hanging over his head. She was sure it was the reason he had called her.

The Copacabana subway station was just over three blocks from her office. It wasn't much for a winter day in Rio de Janeiro. No matter what the weather, Olga liked the walk because it gave her a chance to see what the women in the Zona Sul were wearing, even though she knew that the area wasn't the city's most fashionable and she herself could rarely afford to shop in the nicer stores. She didn't think of herself as pretty, though she knew she had a nice body and an attractive stature, and that her black hair caught the occasional eye.

The office they worked in was small, but it tried, at least from an aesthetic point of view, to imitate American companies. There weren't offices, only a big room filled with linked cubicles that housed three to five people each. It was easy to see if someone was in yet. And Gabriel wasn't. Since he was always the first one in, she was used to the morning ritual of waving and smiling on her way through what he called his stable. The company had around thirty employees; it wouldn't be long before they would run into each other at the coffeemaker or on the way to the bathrooms, which were at the far end of the room.

When a half hour had passed and Gabriel still hadn't appeared, she called his house. A voice answered that could only belong to his mother. She hung up without a word. It was almost ten when he finally arrived; he was slightly out of breath and seemed to be having trouble looking anyone in the eye. He tossed his coat on his desk and, after mumbling something incomprehensible, headed straight for the bathroom. When he emerged a few minutes later, he seemed to be calmer. His hair was wet and combed. Olga approached his desk.

"Are you all right?"

"I am. . . . I was a little late. . . . I needed to take care of a personal matter."

"You don't need to explain. I just want to know if you're okay."

"I'm fine, it's just that I came running from . . ."

"Did something happen?"

"No, thanks, nothing happened. I didn't sleep well."

"Right. If you need any help, just tell me. And thanks for calling last night."

"No problem. Thanks."

They went back to their respective workstations. Gabriel avoided Olga's gaze. There was no longer any doubt about the phone call the night before. It was hard to believe that he was still troubled by the incident with the clairvoyant. She knew it was ridiculous, but she was truly afraid he would carry out the prophecy. She'd known Gabriel ever since she'd started working in that office, and the idea of him killing someone deliberately was entirely absurd. And yet some people were impressionable enough to interpret such a prediction as a call of destiny. And if Gabriel wasn't the kind of person to kill someone, he was clearly someone who was very impressionable.

She tried to concentrate on the technical manual she was editing. Before long she was completely focused on the task of removing an uncomfortable cuticle with her fingernail and thinking back to the birthday party. She wondered whether a prediction could really create an irrepressible impulse. Sensitive people were probably more susceptible to such impulses, and Gabriel was a sensitive person. She liked him. He was the only person in the company she could imagine sleeping with.

⚞

"I still don't get what you want me to do with the boy, Espinosa."

"He's not a boy; he's almost thirty."

"But you make him sound like a boy."

"He seems as vulnerable as a child."

"But this child is announcing a murder."

"He's not the one who's announcing it. It was announced for him."

"And he believed in the prediction to the point that he's asking the police to keep him from pulling the trigger."

"You mean to say that I believe in the prophecy as well."

"You must have a good reason for it."

"Thanks, Welber. I don't have reasons, exactly; I have a feeling about it. Of course I don't believe in astrologers, but I do believe in the power of words, and I have the feeling that this guy is going to get himself in trouble. See what you can do for him. If you think he's crazy and that it's all a fantasy, we'll send him to another precinct."

"The problem is that the only way to know for sure is to wait and see if he kills anybody."

"I don't think it's going to come to that. He'd warn us. If he was really going to kill somebody, he wouldn't have asked."

"I don't like the fact that you gave me this case. He and I are the same age; I think he'd prefer dealing with someone older."

"Welber, I'm not that much older myself. It's not like I'm old enough to be his father."

"It's not your real age that matters. It's what you represent for him. A police sergeant is an authority figure, just like a father."

"Are you dating a psychologist?"

"No, but that's not a bad idea."

Gabriel had left the station a few minutes earlier. From what Espinosa and Welber could make out, the only reason for his visit was reassurance that the officer was taking him seriously. Espinosa's attempt to pass the case on to an assistant hadn't met with Gabriel's favor. He'd been visibly agitated, though he'd done his best to keep a grip on himself; the result of his effort had been a pantomime of random gestures and movements. When Welber was introduced to him, he sat silently for a while, looking at a point between the two officers. Finally he let out a sigh and made a head movement that could have been interpreted as acquiescence. Then, turning toward Espinosa, he asked: "You aren't going to help me anymore?"

"I'm here whenever you need me. I trust Detective Welber completely, and he'll have more time to dedicate to your case. As a sergeant, I'm involved in everything that goes on in this precinct. So he'll be able to help you better than I can."

"I understand. Thank you."

His departure had been almost comical, a mix of hesitation, hurry, and—above all—tension.

The two policemen had exchanged glances, certain that, no matter what they thought about prophecies and psychics, Gabriel's behavior indicated that the prediction was exerting its effect. The question was where it all was heading. Even though Espinosa was interested in the drama of the story, he was still doubtful about how true it was. Not that he doubted Gabriel's suffering: there was no conceivable reason for him to be faking it. But there also was no guarantee that it wasn't just the ravings of a madman, which in no way diminished the possibility of a murder being committed. And he still wasn't sure that Welber was taking any of this seriously. Maybe it was time to start checking out some of the facts the guy had provided. That was an ideal opportunity for Welber to get out of the bureaucratic trap he'd been in for the past year and hit the streets for a real investigation, even though it might just be an investigation into a neurotic's extravagant fantasy.

"Espinosa, I've never heard of anyone going to the police to report an uncommitted murder of an unknown person, especially when the person reporting the murder is the nonmurderer himself."

"Neither have I, but that doesn't mean we should ignore it."

"I think the real threat is to the guy's mental health."

"It could be, but crazy people kill too."

"Let me suggest something. First, let's call the numbers he left and make sure they really belong to him. Then we'll have a friendly conversation with one of his co-workers, preferably the one who introduced the psychic at his birthday. Afterward, we'll talk to his mother and find out what kind of son he is, who his friends are, if there's anything unusual about him, stuff like that. What do you think?"

"For someone who doesn't think much of the story, you're being pretty diligent."

"Like you said, crazy people kill too."

Irene glided smoothly along, head held high, sure that people would get out of her way. That's exactly what happened on Saturday night as she sashayed into the main dining room at Lamas. She was the same height as Olga, but willowier, with a much more attractive face. They had decided to meet at the restaurant in the Largo do Machado, halfway between their houses (even though Irene was driving and her friend had to take the subway). Olga was waiting for her at a table next to a big mirror and waved discreetly when she saw her come in.

Their friendship, dating back to their college days, had endured, even though they'd taken different career paths, and despite the financial gulf between them. They lived in middle-class neighborhoods—Olga in her parents' house, in the Zona Norte of the city, and Irene by herself in the Zona Sul, in Ipanema, one block from the beach. She was a graphic designer in one of the country's largest advertising firms. They kissed each other on the cheek; Irene consulted the big mirror by the table to see if she had attracted any attention from the neighboring tables.

"Sorry to make you come out here on a Saturday night," said Olga.

"I didn't have any plans, and I was dying to see you. Is something the matter?"

"I'm not sure yet. I want to hear what you think, after we have a drink."

After living together for a year—a year that had ended with a difficult separation—they were slowly, carefully trying to reconstruct their original friendship. Olga briefly explained what had happened at Gabriel's birthday, sketched his personality, and described the events following the seer's pronouncement. The story was told over two beers and several fried fish balls, a setting that diluted its drama.

"I don't get what you have to do with it."

"Nothing until now, except a couple of conversations on the subject. Yesterday Gabriel asked me a favor. He wanted to know if I would talk to the sergeant to convince him that he didn't make up the story. Nothing official; it's not a deposition. From what I understand, it's just to say that my friend isn't nuts."

"He might not be nuts, but he sure is weird. A thirty-year-old guy who lives with his mother and tells her everything he does isn't exactly the kind of guy I'd like to be hanging out with next summer."

"He's a good guy—a little shy, but attractive."

"And you want to take the boy from his mother's lap."

"You're making it sound like he's a retard and I'm a child molester."

"That's not important. Are you interested in him?"

"It's not just that. He's really scared, and I want to help him."

"So where do I come in?"

"I'd like you to come with me to meet the sergeant. It doesn't have to be at the station; we can go to a restaurant, a park bench . . ."

"It can be at the station. It's fine with me."

"I knew I could count on you."

"I've always wanted to go to a police station."

At regular intervals, they looked in the mirror to check out their hair, their collars, or the curve their hands made during an expressive gesture. Irene examined herself more often and more meticulously.

"Are you in love with the guy?"

"No, but I'm interested. He's cute. It's complicated, because I work with him. If something bad happened, we'd still have to look at each other every day."

"If everyone thought that way, there'd be more turnover in companies than in cheap motels. If it doesn't work, it doesn't work. You don't have to go into it expecting it to fail. It'd be more worrying if it did work out: how could you look at him at work, on the street, at home, in bed, in the living room, on the bus? If you're interested and if he's cute but shy, you just have to start slowly."

"He's depressed. He really thinks he's going to kill someone."

"And that psychic? Is he real or is he just a fraud?"

"He didn't look like a real astrologer. He seemed to me like someone who likes to prey on naive people."

"How did he end up at the party?"

"He was sitting at the next table. I don't know how he worked his way into the conversation. He had a Spanish accent. What I didn't understand was what good it did him to make predictions like that."

"Maybe later he was going to promise to intercede with the gods."

"I hadn't thought about that. If that happens, Gabriel will definitely fall for it again. It's taken him over completely; he's lost his critical distance."

"This sounds like a case for a psychoanalyst, not for a policeman. Maybe your friend consulted the wrong specialist."

Once Irene had reassured her friend that she would meet with the policeman, the conversation turned to the girls' love lives (especially Irene's). Chats like that happened less frequently than they would have liked. The night ended with the lightheartedness provoked by half a dozen beers.

"You're not ever going to get married again?"

"If the right person comes along, who knows?"

"And who's the right person?"

"That's the problem. We only know when we see them."

"I know exactly what the man I'm going to marry looks like."

"What?"

"He's got to be like you. The way you act, you know? Younger, of course. Not a lot younger. Just a little."

"Let's say . . . twenty years younger?"

"Oh, Espinosa, it doesn't have to be that much. Are you going to like him?"

"Of course."

"He'll have to be good-looking and smart. Like you."

"Much better looking, I should hope."

"He wouldn't have to be. I'd like him to be your height. I'd like him to be the type that doesn't talk a lot, like you. Men who talk a lot aren't very mysterious."

"You know a lot about men for your age."

"I'm thirteen. I'm not a kid anymore. Besides, I go to the movies, I watch TV, and I talk to adults from all over the world on the Internet. I know about more things than you think."

"I'm sure you do."

"Why don't you get a dog, if you're not going to get married? That way you won't be lonely."

"And who's going to take care of him, if I'm all by myself?"

"Me."

"You already have Petita."

"I can walk them both together. Maybe they'll end up getting married."

"I think you think about marriage a lot."

"So?"

"So what?"

"The dog?"

"What dog?"

"What I was talking about. Until you get married. You

don't have to worry. I'll get him at your apartment, walk him, and even give him a bath once a week."

"Thanks. I'll think about it. Actually, I'll think about both things."

"Both what?"

"The dog and getting married."

"Oh, Espinosa."

At least twice a week Alice and Espinosa left at the same time in the morning and walked to the station in animated conversation. Then she continued on to school by herself. They lived on the same floor and they had become friends because their schedules coincided. They had moved quickly from a shy greeting to lively morning conversations; there wasn't much shy about Alice. She was a pretty girl, blond as a Scandinavian and with unmistakably happy blue eyes. Walking beside Espinosa, she felt protected against everything bad in the universe; he felt that her mere existence justified the universe's.

Friday morning. The cases being investigated at the station were moving along. Nothing had happened in the last few days to merit TV or newspaper coverage, which meant that the major crimes were being committed somewhere in the Third World—unthreatening to the small, thin First World of Rio de Janeiro and Copacabana, the area under his jurisdiction. The only news was that Gabriel had asked to come to talk to Espinosa.

"He came here again?" asked Welber.

"No, he called."

"What does he want?"

"I guess he wants to convince us that he's not crazy. That's why he's bringing a colleague who was with him on the night of his birthday party. She'll be a witness to his mental health."

"Maybe that will calm him down."

"I doubt it."

"Do you think he's crazy?"

"Let's just say he's on the verge of a nervous breakdown."

"And?"

"And our conversation is not going to be enough to calm him down."

"What do you think will?"

"From the way things are going, he's only going to calm down when he kills someone."

"Damn, Espinosa, I think you're going overboard."

"Maybe, but I'm starting to think the guy's possessed."

"You think . . ."

"His lifestyle makes it clear that he's not just a regular guy. How crazy he is I'm not sure—I'm not a psychiatrist—but he's got a screw loose; I'm increasingly sure of that. He's always lived within the bounds of normality. But the psychic unleashed the craziness he'd repressed. Now he's sure that he has a destiny he has to fulfill. He's coming to the police not for protection but for an alibi."

"So he's made us characters in his own crazy drama, and we're going along with him toward a murder? And we don't know when or where it's going to be committed."

"Right."

"Do you really believe all of that?"

"For me, it's either that or this guy is just messing with us. And only crazy people screw with the police like that. Either way, he's crazy. All we can do is hope that he's just a nutcase playing with us. If not, he's a nutcase who's about to kill someone."

Dona Alzira had decided to consult Father Crisóstomo about the evil that was clearly infecting Gabriel. Never, not even when her son had been called up for military service—he got out of it because he was the family's breadwinner—had he been caught up in such an intense and obvious crisis. If he was bewitched—and she had no doubt he was—it could only be because of a woman. Not a woman like her, who had retained her virtue since her husband's death, but the devil, disguised as a woman. Infidels had no idea how many forms Lucifer can take. But she knew: she had fought him even when her husband was still alive. She knew all the devil's disguises. And she had no doubt that he was behind Gabriel's sufferings. Maybe Father Crisóstomo could suggest a penance she could fulfill for him, or as a last resort, maybe he could exorcise Gabriel directly. She didn't think it was time for extreme measures: even if he was bewitched, it wasn't quite the same thing as being possessed. Besides, other people couldn't tell what was wrong with him. She was the only one who knew, because nobody knew her son's soul like she did.

She went to mass at the usual time. She knew that she couldn't talk to Father Crisóstomo until after he'd finished the morning service, so she went home to make Gabriel's breakfast—on weekends he slept late—and returned to church after lunch. She brought with her a confection of pumpkin and shredded coconut, one of her specialties and a favorite of Father Crisóstomo's.

"Demonic possession is a very serious thing, my daughter. And very rare. What makes you think that our dear Gabriel is possessed?"

"He seems like a different person, Father Crisóstomo."

"Dona Alzira, young people change a lot when they become adults. I've known Gabriel since the day of his first communion. He was always a nice boy. He's responsible and God-fearing. I've never seen the least sign that he's acting abnormally."

"But he is, Father. I know. I know my son."

"Nobody knows anybody else completely, my daughter. Even those closest to us can surprise us."

"But it's not a surprise, Father. When I say that he's different, I don't mean that something in him changed. I mean he seems like a different person. His body is his, but his soul is somebody else's. God forbid, but it seems like they've changed his soul."

"That's nonsense, Dona Alzira. That can't happen."

"So then what did?"

"He's probably having trouble at work, problems with his girlfriend. . . . It's already high time he started a family. . . . He'd be a good husband and father."

"He's still a boy, Father. He needs to learn more about his work, make some money, and then he can start a family. Anyway, he already has a family. His father died, but he's got me. We're a family."

"Of course you are, Dona Alzira. But I'm talking about the family he's going to start when he gets married and has children. You'll still be a member of the family."

Dona Alzira didn't like one bit the turn the conversation was taking. And she didn't like that Father Crisóstomo wasn't paying enough attention to the fact that Gabriel had been conquered by Satan. What was he talking about, Gabriel getting married? What did that have to do with the way he had changed? If the Church no longer believed in the devil, who did?

"Father, there's nothing I can do? A penance?"

"My child, nobody can do penance for somebody else. You can do penance for your own sins and errors, but not those of anybody else, especially when the other person doesn't even recognize his own sins."

"You don't think anything's happening to him?"

"I didn't say that. It could be that a lot of things are happening to him, and we might even be glad for that. It's part of life. But what I don't think is that he's possessed by the devil. I suggest that you go home and find a moment to talk to your son. You'll see that his demons are a lot less threatening than what you're imagining."

Dona Alzira left visibly annoyed and disappointed. When he'd been younger, Father Crisóstomo hadn't been scared of taking on the devil. He'd even seemed eager to confront the Prince of Darkness in the fight against evil. What she'd just witnessed was a Father Crisóstomo who had given in to age and fear, who was trying to avoid confrontation, who considered ideas of good and evil out-of-date. That was why the Church of Christ was losing ground to drugs and rock music. But she wouldn't go under without a fight. She would struggle for her son's life. She went home thinking over different strategies.

Gabriel wasn't reading or listening to music. He'd simply left, without even writing her a note—another of the countless signs that something had changed radically. There was that girl he worked with, Olga was her name, but it wouldn't do to take the chance of calling someone she'd never met and who might not even know who she was, even though she doubted that Gabriel would have failed to mention his mother to anyone he considered a friend. The way a man treated his mother was the way he showed a woman what kind of man he was. It was unthinkable that her Gabriel wouldn't have mentioned her.

She went to the window, stepped up the little wooden stool, and looked carefully at the people on both sides of the street. She came back down via the stepstool and went into her son's room. She knew all his clothes by heart—she was the one who washed and pressed and sewed them, when necessary—and by process of elimination figured out what pants and shirt he was wearing that day, which scarf and which shoes. She decided that he had dressed as if he were going to work. But he didn't work on Saturdays. The company never asked its employees for overtime, at least not as long as Gabriel had been working there. There was no doubt. Gabriel had gone out to meet someone.

The dismissive way Father Crisóstomo had treated her story left her feeling more helpless than she had felt at any point since her husband's death. And her sense of helplessness deepened when she realized that not even her husband, when he was alive, would have been the right person to handle this kind of problem. That was when the phone rang. She immediately assumed it was Gabriel, excusing himself for not leaving a note.

"Hello?" inquired a somewhat timid female voice at the other end of the line.

"Hello, yes."

"Yes, I'd like to speak to Gabriel, please."

"He's not here. Who's calling?"

"It's a friend of his. . . . I'll call later. . . . Thank you."

"You don't want to leave your name?"

"Thanks . . . I'm not sure he'll remember. . . . Thanks. Good-bye."

Dona Alzira took the phone call as yet another small sign that something out of the ordinary was going on with her son. Even worse: if that little woman was calling, that meant that he wasn't going out with her. It meant he was meeting *another* woman. She was sure she'd never heard that voice before. She knew all the people who called Gabriel. Not them, necessarily, but their voices. And yet she was sure of one thing. If the person didn't want to leave a message, not even her name, it was because she wanted to remain anonymous, and nobody made a point of hiding their name unless they had something else to hide. She left her son's room and went back to the little steps that made up her observation post. Two things bothered her intensely: the evil that was attacking her son and the loss of Father Crisóstomo's support. Ever since Serafim's death, Father Crisóstomo had been her counselor in everything that had to do with Gabriel. And just when she most needed his help, he'd hesitated, played coy. She hoped that it was just a passing phase: a symptom of age rather than a weakness of faith.

She would turn sixty when her son turned thirty, in the same month. Their birthdays were only a week apart. She'd dreamed of having a party together, with all their friends and relatives. There was the problem of finding a place: the little apartment in Flamengo wouldn't even fit all their relatives (and there weren't that many of them), not to mention her son's colleagues and friends. In any case, there was nothing to celebrate. She wasn't even sure that she and her son would make it to their birthdays safe and sound.

***

All he wanted to do was make sure that the man was real, that he walked and talked like any other inhabitant of the city, that he wasn't some kind of supernatural spirit hovering above common mortals. What he found out about him—to his surprise—was that on Saturday and Sunday afternoons he could be found in some of the chain restaurants that had spaces for children's parties. The man who gave him the information wasn't sure what he did at those parties; Gabriel found out later that he put on marionette plays with his girlfriend's help—or maybe it was the other way around, and he helped her. He couldn't imagine that sinister figure having anything to do with a children's party, least of all performing with a puppet theater. Gabriel had spent three weekends casing out the hamburger joints of the Zona Sul looking for the Argentine. He didn't know his name or where he came from; all he knew from his accent was that he was from some Spanish-speaking country. Argentina was Gabriel's own invention. He thought of Argentines the same way he thought about gypsies: always suspicious. There were parties in several restaurants, but he didn't find any trace of the psychic in any of them. He didn't know what he would do if he found him. He didn't even know if he really wanted to find him. He himself felt suspect walking into the children's party rooms; nobody knew him, and all eyes—especially those of the birthday child's parents—were on him. The look was questioning and yet friendly, as if they were thanking him for coming and trying to figure out who he was. Occasionally they would even give him a sandwich and a soft drink. He didn't know what crime he was committing, but he was sure he was committing one: breaking and entering, perjury, unlawful seizure, theft. He almost always left with his head down, ashamed, excusing himself.

Since he didn't have a car and didn't have the money to hire a taxi to take him around on Saturday and Sunday afternoons, he had to focus his investigation on the restaurants along the bus routes, disembarking every time he saw one. His search was irregular and disorganized. On the first weekend he covered Flamengo, Catete, and Largo do Machado, all on foot. On the second weekend, with a little more difficulty, he took in the neighborhoods of Botafogo and Urca, which, since the route wasn't linear, involved changing buses several times. When he went through Copacabana and Ipanema, the search became qualitatively simpler but quantitatively much more arduous, since there were so many more restaurants. Toward the end, he had the sense that he was going to the same party over and over again, with the same children, the same parents, the same decorations, the same clowns. It was almost enough to make him forget what he was looking for.

He was haunted day and night—not by the face of the seer, but by the curse, pronounced with a slight Spanish accent. In fact, the actual way the psychic had said it had long since changed into a cold and impersonal statement, like a death sentence. Gabriel didn't have visions. He didn't have fantasies about killing someone. He didn't dream about deaths and murders. He was terrorized by a simple phrase: the sentence the Argentine had spoken, and that alone. No visual images accompanied it. Only the sounds: the Argentine's voice, with its slight Spanish accent. On the way from his ears to his brain, the sound had come alive in the interior of his head. The mere recollection of the tone of voice was enough to make him dizzy. His scalp felt sweaty.

During his trip back home he realized that the Argentine might live in the Zona Norte, or even in some distant suburb. That would turn his search into a lottery, and he didn't think he was the lucky type. Carless and clueless, he could spend the rest of his days trolling through the children's birthday parties of Rio de Janeiro.

He felt like a complete idiot, not only because of the fruitless search that had swallowed up his last three weekends but because he didn't know what he was looking for or why he was looking for it. What would he do if he found the Argentine? Try to attack him? But he had never been the aggressive type. The aggression had been in the man's prophecy, and that, he had to admit, had been spoken in a firm tone but with a soft voice. What would he try to get the psychic to do? Change his prophecy? That would not only be idiotic, it would be ridiculous.

He got off the bus at Flamengo Beach, breaking habit by entering his street from that end, not, as usual, from the Rua do Catete. He had to walk a good ways before making out the facade of his building and his mother's silhouette against the light of the window. She certainly would have felt him coming long before she actually saw him.

He responded with a grunt to his mother's message about the phone call from the unknown woman and locked himself in his room. He only turned on the lamp, and even that felt excessive, but he didn't feel right in complete night. It had already made him walk too far; where would he have lunch? He was almost to the Avenida Atlântica when he retraced his steps. A few moments later, he found himself in front of a girl who was looking at him sympathetically and asking, "To go?" In response to his nod, she slid the sandwich and milkshake into a paper bag.

Back at the station, he got yet another call from Gabriel, asking if their meeting could take place at the end of the next day, around five in the afternoon, a time that would be convenient for them.

"Chief, has it occurred to you that the kid might be running some kind of scam?"

"What scam, Welber? There's no scam. We don't even have a case."

When Welber left his office, Espinosa couldn't help thinking about what he'd said. Indeed, since the very first phone call, and more specifically since their first meeting in the restaurant, Gabriel had been in charge of the itinerary. He had assigned everyone involved a role, as if he were writing a story. On the other hand, he didn't feel as if the guy was manipulating him. He didn't even think that was what the guy was trying to do, at least not consciously. In any case, he would be more careful. His own fantasies were enough trouble. He didn't need any extra confusion.

He went back home at his regular time and, as usual, stopped off for a few minutes at the store, where he bought black bread, cold cuts, and drinks. In the winter he usually

darkness. He slowly removed his clothes, weighing every movement, precisely extending his arms and legs within the tiny space available to him.

He heard the movements of his mother preparing dinner. He wasn't hungry. The smell of food reminded him of the countless sweets and hot dogs he'd encountered in the fast-food places; it made him sick. He tried to resist the impulse to bite his nails, an irritating habit he'd acquired a few weeks ago. But that wasn't what annoyed him the most. If he could place everything that annoyed him in a well-defined hierarchy, his mother's controlling attitude would be at the very top. His impatience with her had begun around two or three years ago, provoked by a few unimportant episodes. As his irritation grew, they grew further apart. Their physical contact had stopped when he was still a child. Besides functional everyday talk, they rarely had a conversation. He refrained from biting his nails, but he noticed that his hands were sweaty, despite the cool air coming through the half-opened window. He turned off the lamp and let the streetlight illuminate his room. He stretched out in bed, without moving, waiting for his mother to knock on the door to tell him that dinner was ready.

❧

Monday began slowly, after a listless weekend. The alarm clock didn't ring, a fact Espinosa attributed to a mechanical failure rather than his own failure to set it. He got to the station late, having missed his chance to talk to Alice. Welber was waiting for him.

"Your friend Gabriel called, insisting on bringing a coworker here to talk to you at the station."

"Welber—"

"It won't work. He said it has to be with you. And he asked if it could be at the end of the day, after they get off work."

"Who's 'they'?"

"Him and his coworker."

"Girlfriend?"

"I don't know. He says she was there at the birthday party."

"All right. Did you find out anything about the Argentine?"

"Not even the guy, Gabriel, knows if he's Argentine. He could be from any country in South America. He could be a Brazilian trying to sound like a foreigner. In any case, we haven't found a record of anyone who matches the boy's description."

"Welber, he's not a boy, he's just a guy who's scared."

"Fuck, Espinosa. Our job isn't comforting frightened children."

⌁

Episodes like this one broke up the monotony of his job, which was increasingly dominated by paper-pushing. The cop who investigated crimes and tracked down thieves was a less familiar figure. Robberies and murders were on the

rise, but they weren't the main focus of police work country marked by huge income disparities, the only job of the police was to keep the Third World from i ing the First. Espinosa knew this; a few other colle knew it; the rest of the force was composed of peop shady as the ones they arrested, attacked, and shook d Against such a backdrop, a man threatened by a fort teller with committing murder was certainly a chang pace.

The rest of the morning passed in a blizzard of p Espinosa left for lunch without having decided whe go; there were several options within easy walking tance. A fine haze filtered and spread the sunlight; light was brilliant. Buildings, trees, people, and obj were perfectly lit: strongly illuminated and free of shac Espinosa also noticed a man with one shoe that was sh and clean and another that was dirty and beat up. In f this was more interesting to him than the light; unlike ural events, this one involved a story. Why would some wear one dirty shoe and one clean one? It wasn't, thought as he walked beyond the couple of blocks wh he ordinarily ate lunch, it wasn't and it couldn't be t he'd walked through a puddle or accidentally stuck his f in something. The shoe wasn't accidentally dirty; it h been systematically mistreated. What kind of pers would dedicate special attention to one shoe while letti the other fall to pieces? The enigma had no importance f anyone besides the shoes' owner himself, but it was food f many hours of thought; it might even keep Espinosa up preferred red wine to beer: it was more elegant, and better for the heart. Lately, he'd been trying to substitute a snack for a full meal, occasionally allowing himself some canned soup as an appetizer. It was all part of his effort to reduce his domestic duties to a bare minimum. He'd long considered the oven a prehistoric relic. But he hadn't yet managed to eliminate plates, cups, and silverware. He couldn't stand eating with plastic utensils.

Alice was sitting on the bench in front of the building, while Petita, who had nothing petite about her, was watching the movements of a ball being tossed around by a group of children. Girl and dog moved toward Espinosa as soon as they saw him approaching.

"I'm so glad you've arrived. I've got news. A litter has been born. Two males and three females."

"What are you talking about, honey?"

"About your dog, of course."

"What dog?"

"A Labrador."

"A what?"

"A Labrador. You don't know what a Labrador is?"

"A dog breed."

"Right. Didn't we agree that you were lonely and that you needed a dog?"

"We didn't agree any such thing. You're the one who decided that."

"But you didn't disagree."

"Which doesn't mean I agreed."

"Espinosa, they're wonderful. The color of sand. The owner of the litter says I can have first pick."

Petita, a pointer whose main way of relating to the world was sniffing, was trying to discover, with the tip of her nose, what was in the shopping bags.

"They were born the day before yesterday. They're so, so cute."

"I can imagine."

"And the owner said that pointers and Labradors get along perfectly."

"And what is this human here going to do with a Labrador?"

"You don't have to do anything. He's the one who will take care of you. He'll be your friend, he'll sleep next to you, he'll be wagging his tail whenever you come home, he'll protect your apartment . . ."

"And who is going to take care of him?"

"I already said I'll take care of him. I'll take him on walks, bathe him, take him to the vet, everything. On Saturday I'll take you there to see them. It's right here in the Peixoto District. They have to stay with their mother until they can be weaned. So you've got time to choose. Don't say anything until you've seen them."

Espinosa leaned over to give her two little kisses, which she took as a sign that her plan was moving forward.

❦

Olga's first thought upon awaking was of her meeting with the police sergeant that afternoon. She'd never been to a police station before, and the images she'd seen on the TV news weren't encouraging. Luckily, Irene had agreed to come along. Gabriel would be there, but she suspected that he would be needing a lot of support. And she was a little worried because she didn't know exactly what they wanted from her. Gabriel had said it wasn't to give a deposition; it wasn't anything official, just an informal conversation to convince the sergeant that he wasn't making up the whole story. But wasn't he? Could she swear that ninety percent of what was happening was anything more than his own invention? Besides, nothing *was* happening, except for his neurotic anxieties and fantasies. As for the rest, there was the fortune-teller's prediction, but that in itself was a bunch of nonsense. She drank her coffee thinking that if she was lucky she'd run into Gabriel in the subway station. That way they'd have a couple of minutes to chat about the meeting. Gabriel had asked her not to mention it at work; it could have negative consequences.

She didn't see Gabriel on the platform at Catete, where he usually got on the train; but in the Copacabana station, as she was walking toward the escalators, she felt a hand on her shoulder. It was him.

"I looked for you at your station," said Olga.

"I got in the last car, right when the train was about to leave."

"Is the meeting this afternoon still on?"

"Yes . . . You're coming, right?"

"I am. I asked a girlfriend to come with me. I think I'll

feel better with her. I imagine there are a lot of smarmy men in a police station."

"It's not like that at all. It's a public place—you don't have to be scared. Who's your friend?"

"Her name is Irene. We've been friends since college. Don't worry about her; she can take care of herself."

It was only a little more than three blocks from the train station to the building where they worked. They walked the last two in silence. Gabriel walked with his eyes on the sidewalk. Occasionally, he looked at Olga and smiled awkwardly. They looked like two strangers in an elevator.

The few times they ran into each other throughout the rest of the day were marked by Gabriel's complete unease. At five o'clock, as arranged, they left for the station. They talked about the weather, making the cold seem worse than it really was, and arrived at the station without any uncomfortable silences. As soon as they walked in the station's entrance, Gabriel started babbling nervously. Olga took his arm, and by the time they reached the second floor he seemed to have calmed down. A detective asked them to wait; the sergeant was tied up on an urgent matter. They sat on the sofa next to the stairs and waited for fifteen minutes; just as Sergeant Espinosa opened the door of his office, Irene arrived at the top of the stairs, and he saw Olga introduce Irene to Gabriel. Then it was Gabriel's turn to introduce the girls to the officer, which he did rather uncomfortably. Espinosa invited them into his office. The peaceful gaze he directed at each of them before they sat down lingered a few seconds on Irene.

"Sergeant, thank you for seeing me once again. I thought it was important that you listen to my colleague, Olga, who was there at my birthday party. Irene here is a friend of Olga's."

Olga looked at Gabriel with surprise. During the entire day, he'd hardly managed to get out a single coherent phrase, and here he was, speaking articulately, using precise words, almost eloquent. Gabriel noticed the effect of his words and tried to play it down.

"I'm sorry about how formal I sound. It's because you haven't met the girls yet, sir. . . . I don't even know one of them—"

"But you don't seem shy in the least," Irene interrupted.

"What?"

"Nothing. Just a conversation Olga and I had."

Gabriel looked at Olga questioningly. She quickly clarified her friend's words.

"When I asked Irene to come with me, I tried to bring her up to speed on what was going on and I mentioned you. . . . I think I might have said that you're a little shy."

"Ah."

"But she also said you're interesting," Irene added.

After Irene's observation, there was a little bit of doubt in the air about what exactly she meant. Olga was clearly beginning to question the wisdom of bringing her along. Espinosa still hadn't said a word.

"Sergeant, the reason I asked my colleague to come here with me was so that she could convince you that I'm telling the truth."

"But I never doubted your word."

"Yes, I know . . . but I thought I should reinforce it. . . . If she could tell you . . ."

"Of course she can. I'd be happy to hear what you have to say."

Before Olga could start the story, Irene addressed Espinosa.

"Sergeant . . ."

"Espinosa."

"Sergeant Espinosa, I don't have anything to say about what happened; I don't even really know what happened. I'm just here with my friend . . ."

Irene was visibly taken with the officer. Olga was pleased by this turn of events, as it meant she wasn't focusing her attention on Gabriel.

Gabriel was starting to get impatient.

"If you could listen to my colleague . . ."

"Of course I can; that's why you came, after all. Please, Miss."

Olga was disconcerted by the lack of importance the officer seemed to be granting the visit. Except, of course, Irene's presence.

"I don't know exactly what you want to know, sir."

"Don't worry about what I want to know. Focus on what you want to tell me."

"All right." She looked at Gabriel as if asking for help; she looked at Irene, who was looking at Espinosa, and then began relating the events at Gabriel's birthday party. The story didn't vary much from the version he himself had told, except that she didn't emphasize the Argentine's phrases as much as he had. As she spoke, Gabriel's eyes were fixed on Espinosa, as if he were awaiting some more explicit statement, maybe some kind of declaration. When she finished, he couldn't contain himself anymore.

"So?"

Nothing.

"What do you think, sir?"

Espinosa remained silent, a silence that didn't last more than a few seconds but that, because of the kid's anxiety, seemed like long minutes.

"I think it's perfectly compatible with what you told me."

"So you believe me?"

"If I didn't believe you, we wouldn't be sitting here. What you don't seem to understand is that the fact that I believe your story doesn't mean I also have to believe that the Argentine's prediction is going to come true. Dona Olga, have you ever seen the Argentine before?"

"No. I didn't even know he was from Argentina."

"Neither do we."

"And you, Miss . . ."

"Please don't call me Miss . . . just Irene. No. I only learned about this situation a couple of days ago, in the middle of so much beer that I can't even keep all the names straight. Until a few minutes ago I didn't know if Espinosa was the name of the cop or the fortune-teller. If I may say so, Espinosa seems like a better name for a psychic than for a policeman."

"Sometimes we try to be psychic."

"Sorry, Officer. But I don't know what I'm supposed to be doing here. I'm worried; I'm not good at sitting on the sidelines."

"There's no reason to drag out this conversation. There's nothing here that justifies an investigation. The supposed Argentine didn't charge for what he did. He didn't force anybody to listen to him. And according to what you've both told me, he was calm and respectful. So what do you want me to charge him with?" he said, looking at Gabriel. "The only person who can be accused of anything is you, in the event the prediction comes true."

Gabriel's face was frozen, his eyes glassy. His lips were pressed together; he looked as if he was about to collapse.

"Officer, my friend is very nervous," Olga said. "He can't concentrate at work, he doesn't talk to anybody in the office, he seems sick. . . . It's true that the fortune-teller was polite and friendly, but I was there, and I have to say that he shocked me and all our friends. . . . But nobody else took it seriously, maybe because they were too nervous to think about it. I guess Gabriel took it more seriously than anybody else, but after all the prediction was about him."

"I understand your point of view completely. But I'd like you to try to understand mine. I am a police sergeant. I don't have any jurisdiction over people's imaginations. I don't have a single concrete fact to begin an investigation with. Unless he gets in touch with Gabriel and offers to undo the prediction with a sum of money . . . For now the most concrete thing we have is the psychological effect of a prediction on a person's mind. There's no more or less truth to it than there is in the prophecies of the fire-and-brimstone preachers on the street corner. As for the possibility that Gabriel could kill somebody, it only depends on whether he wants to confirm the fortune-teller's prophecy or give it the lie."

"You mean . . . you mean . . . that you're closing the case?"

"I'm not closing the case. The case was never opened. All there was were a couple of conversations between the two of us, and my offer to see you whenever you wanted to talk to us. The offer, and our availability, remain open."

The daylight had diminished, and the light on Espinosa's desk was proving inadequate. Along with the light, Gabriel's spirits were growing dimmer and dimmer as the meeting wound its way to the end. The lamplight picked out the holster and gun that Espinosa had left on the desk. That's where Gabriel's gaze finally came to rest. Espinosa put the gun in a drawer, got up, and turned on the overhead light. The encounter ended with Espinosa's request that they all write down their names and telephone numbers on a piece of paper, in case he needed to get in touch with any of them.

When they said their farewells, the officer made a point of walking them out. Irene generously returned Espinosa's gaze and handshake, certain that his asking for their names and numbers was just a strategy to get hers. On the sidewalk in front of the station, Gabriel blinked nervously and sought out Olga's hand. It was clear that he was unhappy with having Irene there. Together, they all walked toward the subway station. He was sure that the meeting's failure was Irene's fault. When Olga took his hand, it felt dead.

The manager of the luncheonette gave the message to Hidalgo, who went muttering back to his partner.

"Just like yesterday. Someone's looking for us."

"Any idea who?"

"No, but it doesn't sound like somebody who wants a puppet show for their kid."

"Could it be somebody you promised to help?"

"Maybe. I just can't think who."

"You can't mix up your puppet clients with your fortune-telling. I bet you don't even remember what you tell people. Eventually you're going to slip up and they're going to realize it's all a farce."

"What farce, woman? It's not a farce. I always tell the truth, because people always ask the same things: if they're going to have money, health, and love. In that order."

"I don't like this, having people looking for us. It could be the tax man. It could be the cops."

"Nonsense. We're not criminals."

"I'm scared."

"Get a grip. You're scared of traffic guards. Get the dolls ready. I'm going to get us some sandwiches and soft drinks."

Hidalgo crossed the McDonald's party room as if he were gliding through a salon in a royal palace. The children, who were bawling and running in every direction, didn't exist; even the adults were ignored. If they didn't get out of the way, he would have walked right through them. And yet children and adults, men and women, were transfixed by his looks, his demeanor. Stella, his girlfriend, assistant, and business partner, was very pretty, but she wasn't quite as alluring, perhaps because she spoke in a slightly vulgar way or because, compared to her boyfriend, there was nothing outstanding about the way she carried herself.

"We're ready whenever you want to start. The kids are getting impatient," said the birthday boy's mother, looking dreamily at Hidalgo.

"Of course, ma'am. As soon as we're finished eating we guarantee you half an hour of silence and peace. Ours will be the only voices heard."

And that's exactly what happened. By the time the prince announced his intention to rescue the princess, the children had their eyes glued on the small stage where the little puppets were obeying Hidalgo and Stella's commands. After their presentation, it was time to sing "Happy Birthday," for the birthday boy to blow out his candles, and for the parents to distribute the plastic-wrapped slices of cake. It was time for Hidalgo to say farewell to the parents and to offer some extra services.

"Congratulations, ma'am. Your son is a beautiful child. I foresee a wonderful future for him. He'll be perfectly able to overcome the obstacles that come his way."

"What do you mean, obstacles? Do you see something bad in his future? Are you a psychic?"

"I'm occasionally able to foresee isolated incidents in a person's future, though I can't control this capacity."

Screaming disrupted his communication with the young mother. He had chosen his moment strategically.

"I'm not sure what you mean."

"Don't worry about it. I'm just congratulating you and your son."

"But what do you mean by obstacles? Health problems? Money?"

"It's not too clear. While we were performing I was busy with the voices and the puppets, and after that all the kids started running around and shouting. . . ."

"Maybe in different circumstances. Do you have a phone?"

"Unfortunately not, but if you give me your number I'll get in touch."

She wrote her name, Maria Clara, on a paper napkin; underneath she added "mother of Eduardo (Duda)." Hidalgo took advantage of the arrival of one of the children's mothers to say good-bye and move on. Stella had taken apart the little stage and packed up the puppets and equipment into two bags.

"Here, keep this."

"What is it?"

"Didn't you want to organize our clients? Well, you can add Duda's mother to the list. She's anxious to know if he's going to be rich and healthy."

"Be careful. It could end up costing us the money for the performance."

"We're not going to lose anything, sweetie. We're going to make more. A lot more. We need a place to see clients. It's not a good idea to do it at home. It's about time we start reaping what we've sown."

"I just want you to be careful. Don't forget, I work for the government. I can't afford to lose my job."

"Like you said, it's a job, not work. Now we're going to have to get to work. With our heads."

It was the end of the afternoon. Hidalgo and Stella left the restaurant. She was carrying the bags; he looked like he was waiting for the chauffeur to bring around the limo.

He turned the corner without noticing Gabriel entering the McDonald's.

Gabriel hadn't talked to Olga since the encounter at the police station. In order to avoid her, he tried to arrive at and leave the office at irregular times. He didn't say more than "Hi" or "How's it going" when she visited his part of the floor and peered over his partition. Nor had he called the station again. He didn't want to talk to the detective who had been assigned to take care of him; clearly, the fellow didn't have any professional experience. And he certainly didn't have enough life experience. Olga had deeply, perhaps irrevocably, disappointed him by bringing Irene along. Had she not understood how serious the situation was? Didn't she comprehend the enormity of the tragedy that was taking hold of him? Had it been his mistake, failing to realize that Olga couldn't distinguish between a tragedy and an everyday event?

In the three days since the meeting, Gabriel had retreated into himself. Or at least he'd tried. He'd been educated by Augustinians, and in grade school the brothers taught him how, in moments of crisis, when the exterior world became impossible, to reach deep inside himself. The truth is not outside of us, they said. Why hadn't he looked inside himself to make sense of the Argentine's prediction? Why the sergeant? Could it be that his once-acute ability to discern good people from bad was becoming dulled? That Irene was disqualified. It was clear the moment he'd first set eyes on her. The sergeant, though he seemed like a good enough person, was a man, and, as far as Gabriel could tell, single. Irene picked up on it immediately. Women knew those things. She was certainly an attractive woman. Her eyes pierced his soul like the nails that pierced the crucified Christ. Maybe he was mixing things up. What did Christ have to do with this? It was a police station, not a church. That's why he'd asked the officer if they could meet outside the station. Places polluted people. Nobody could avoid thinking about God in the middle of a church. And nobody could avoid thinking about evil in the middle of a police station. Including, of course, the officer himself. It was naive to imagine that Espinosa, the very man who reigned over that environment, could get to the truth of the matter. He'd given up searching for the truth in order to play the seduction game with Irene. The idea that Gabriel could seek external help was an illusion.

It had all started with the Argentine's prediction. He'd have to keep looking for him. That was the only way he could change the course of events, if indeed it could be altered. He remembered distinctly that there were no conditions attached to the prediction. Like all true divinations, it was an imperative. This was the point he wanted to clear up with the Argentine: was it a vision, the particulars of which could be open to interpretation, or did it refer to an unalterable, divinely foreordained event? Another thing he would have to look into was whether Espinosa's transformation was just a mood or a definitive change.

The mere idea that there was nothing he could do to prevent the murder made him shaky. He could not remain at the mercy of other people's romantic whims. He'd have to act. Which meant, first, finding the Argentine. And, second, arming himself. He couldn't stand the idea of carrying a weapon any more than he could stand the idea of using one against a fellow human being. But if he was going to meet the Argentine, he would have to have a way to defend himself.

❧

Dona Alzira had been looking for Father Crisóstomo for a week. She'd let time go by. In the meantime, unhurriedly, she had thought about the Father's words, about how little interest he'd shown both in Gabriel's problem and in her own suffering.

She'd taken the opportunity of her son's absence to check whether any of his clothes needed mending. On top of the single bed she had divided shirts, pants, underwear, socks, and coats into piles; the suit jackets hung from the handles of the built-in wardrobe. Dona Alzira made major decisions while carrying out such work. In fact, sometimes it seemed as if she chose to examine her son's clothes (it used to be her husband's clothes) precisely at the moment that she needed to confront an important choice in her life. Until she'd reached a decision, she didn't consider her work complete. And if there were no more buttons to sew on, she would sew the old buttons on even more firmly. She had never put the clothes back into the closet without having resolved her problem.

Her son had left for yet another one of those mysterious weekend excursions. She didn't dare ask what he was up to on Saturday and Sunday afternoons. He always came home by dusk. So it was something that happened only in the afternoon, never in the morning or at night, which, in her opinion, excluded several possibilities, especially trysts with women, which she imagined to be exclusively nocturnal. She considered the possibility that he had taken on some extra weekend job, but it seemed unthinkable that he would have done so without telling her. Unless it was to surprise her. A while back he'd mentioned buying a car—secondhand, of course; they could take little day trips, and even short vacations. But Gabriel wasn't acting like someone who was about to surprise her, at least not in the way she had in mind. Her attempts to get him to talk had had no effect. To the contrary: he'd clammed up even more.

The afternoon was coming to an end; the mending had all been done; Dona Alzira was taking the clothes back into Gabriel's room—and she still had no idea what to do. Her only certainty was that she was not going to stand by idly while her son was destroyed.

If her son wasn't going to talk, if Father Crisóstomo wouldn't pay her any mind, there was only one thing to do: follow Gabriel and find out what was going on. The next day was Sunday.

⋘

Espinosa's Saturday began with the same impasse that always marked his Saturdays: of all the things around the house that needed to be done, which should he attack first? Organize the books that were accumulating along the wall of the living room? A while back, he'd started to assemble a shelfless bookshelf. He'd lined up the books in a row, as he would on a regular bookshelf, except that in his version the "shelves" were made up of books laid horizontally along the top of the first row. Then he'd arranged another vertical row of books on top of the horizontal layer, and so on. The bookcase, which already occupied an entire wall of his living room, had grown taller than he was, a clear sign that the problem itself was now bigger than he was. Did it really need to be resolved? Or was it best to abandon it to its fate? That is, should he, Espinosa, await the day when the books were piled so high that the equilibrium would shatter and the whole thing would come crashing down?

This was only one of the many dilemmas that greeted his Saturday mornings. There was also the question of the appliances that were nearing total breakdown, including the washing machine. If it kept moving around every time he used it, it would end up on the other side of the living room, on the little balcony, where it could enjoy the view over the square. There was the toaster, which toasted only one side of the bread, doubling the time necessary to complete the operation. Then there was the iron, and the lamp on his bedside table. He'd resolved to leave the carpentry and plumbing problems for his next vacation. With such a wide range of problems requiring urgent solutions, he decided that the best thing would be to calmly peruse the newspapers in order not to be forced to any hurried conclusion. Then the doorbell rang.

There weren't a lot of people who could bring a smile to his face on Saturday morning, before he'd had time to read the papers. The little creature he encountered at the door was one of them.

"Hi, how are you? Well, ready to go?"

"Ready to go where?"

"Espinosa! Don't tell me you forgot!"

"God help me, sweetheart . . . but if you give me a

hint . . ." The disappointed expression was magnified by two enormous blue eyes that stared attentively, awaiting his answer. Espinosa forced himself to remember.

"The puppies."

Alice threw her arms around his neck with all the spontaneity that her thirteen years allowed her.

"You don't think it's kind of early? Maybe the owners of the puppies are still asleep."

"Don't worry. I already went by and they're up. I took Petita for her walk and I went to have a look. Do you want some time to shave and change clothes?"

"I can't go like this?"

"Oh, Espinosa. I'll come by in half an hour, all right?"

"All right, I'll put on my special puppy-visiting outfit."

Half an hour later, they were walking up one of the streets that surrounded the Peixoto District.

"Espinosa."

"Speaking."

"You said you were married."

"That's right."

"What was your wife like?"

"She was great. She was with me in law school. We got married as soon as I graduated. She graduated two years later."

"Was she pretty?"

"She was. She probably still is: she's only forty."

"Older than my mom."

"Your mother and she are both still young."

"Did you have kids?"

"We had one. He's two years older than you."

"You don't ever see him?"

"Rarely. He lives in the United States, in Washington. He only comes to Brazil once a year."

"Don't you miss him?"

"I do. And I think he misses me too."

"Did his mother get remarried?"

"She did."

"Is that why she went to the United States?"

"That's right. She married someone who works at the Brazilian embassy in Washington."

"Why did your marriage end?"

"It was my fault."

"What did you do?"

"It's less what I did, honey, and more what I stopped doing."

To Espinosa's surprise, Alice didn't ask any more questions. She seemed to understand his reply.

The building they were going to was in the highest part of the neighborhood. The apartment was on the ground floor, with a large covered patio at the back. A foreign-looking woman spoke with Alice as if they'd known each other their whole lives. She greeted Espinosa with excessive respect when Alice introduced him as "my friend Sergeant Espinosa." The puppies were in the covered patio. The mother, lying on her side, napped while the five puppies fought over her teats. She opened her eyes to examine the visitors, gave a slight wag of her tail when Alice called her name, and got up, two puppies still dangling off her stomach. Alice, already on intimate terms with all of them—woman, mother, and puppies—took a sand-colored male, let the mother take a sniff, and passed him to Espinosa.

"This is yours. He still doesn't have a name."

Espinosa looked at the owner and held the little Labrador in his cupped hands. The baby still smelled of milk; he immediately started to lick Espinosa's fingers.

"So?" Alice's eyes were bright.

"He's very sweet."

"In another month you can take him home."

"But . . ."

"I already told you I'd take care of him. You don't have to worry about anything. I'll walk him, bathe him, take him to the vet. All you have to do is like him." She shot a meaningful glance at the owner, and both looked at Espinosa.

Alice talked the whole way back about the advantages of the Labrador breed.

"Espinosa, they're the dogs they use to lead the blind."

"You think I'm—"

"I know you're not blind, even though you don't always get everything."

"What do you mean?"

"Nothing. Let's pick out a name for him."

Before they got back to the building, several dozen names had already been proposed.

"Since he's always going to be a little bit here and a little bit there, why don't we call him Neighbor?" Espinosa proposed.

"Great. We're neighbors and he's our Neighbor. I like it."

"So that's that. What I still haven't figured out is how I'm going to keep a dog if I'm away all day. But according to you that's not a problem. He can wag his tail for me on the weekends and destroy my apartment from Monday to Friday."

They decided to meet at the same restaurant as last week. Again, when Irene arrived, Olga was already seated, at the same table. She was working on her first beer and looking around in expectation. Like the first time, she waved when she saw her friend enter the hallway leading to the Lamas Room—and once again Irene proved that she was able to attract almost every eye in a crowded room.

"At last we get to talk about the meeting."

"Thanks so much for coming with us. It was horrible. I'm so embarrassed that I brought you along."

"But Olga, I loved it! And that officer . . . What a waste. A man like that, surrounded by crooks."

"I thought you—"

"I had a great time. Your guy isn't bad either. A little pale for my taste, but nothing some fun on the beach won't fix. I just didn't understand what he wanted with the officer. Nobody did anything wrong. What's the real problem?"

"I just don't know anymore. I'm really confused. I

thought that by going along with him to the meeting I could help Gabriel, but I think I just made things worse."

"But you didn't do a thing. You hardly spoke. Now: your guy said exactly—"

"He's not my guy. Ever since that day, he's gotten even weirder. He doesn't speak to anyone at the office, and even when he has to go to the bathroom he's careful to choose a moment when he won't run into anybody on the way. I think he's going nuts."

"Or he always was and nobody noticed."

"No. He was cheerful. It's true he wasn't chatty, but he never avoided his coworkers. He was always so nice to me. Everything changed on the day that fucking psychic told him he was going to kill someone. *That* guy is nuts. And aggressive. Son of a bitch."

"Calm down, sweetie. As far as I know, nobody goes to jail for being a son of a bitch. There wouldn't be enough people left to arrest them. Look at the situation again. One. A small group from the office is celebrating a birthday. Two. A guy nobody knows comes up and offers to tell the birthday boy's fortune. Three. Besides the standard predictions, he foresees that the guy is going to kill somebody before his next birthday. Four. The birthday boy gets desperate and calls the cops. Five. This whole thing is insane."

"I know it's insane, Irene. The officer must think so too. And that's what everyone should think, but it's not how Gabriel sees it. He *is* desperate. I have no idea why, but he thinks the guy was telling the truth. I get the impression that Gabriel considers the murder already done. Now he's just waiting for the day to arrive."

"Then, my dear, your guy really is bananas."

"But that's just the point. He isn't. He's a hard worker, he does his job well, he speaks articulately, he's smart. . . ."

"I didn't say he's always going to be crazy, or that he's always been crazy. I just mean that for the time being he is going through a period of being crazy. My question is: why did that Argentine's prediction drive him nuts? If some guy in a bar told me something like that, I'd tell him to go fuck himself. Or I'd say he was right and tell him I'd kill him. I think that's what any reasonably normal person would do. Why is he so different?"

"Gabriel's the dreamy type. At least that's the impression I get. But he always had a grip on reality."

"Everybody does, honey. If they didn't, they wouldn't believe in eternal love and knights in shining armor. You'll see. He was wanting someone to die. And then this sorcerer shows up and tells him exactly what he was already thinking . . . and bam! The guy gets worse."

"Maybe. I think he'd be susceptible in that case."

"The question is then, did the Argentine guy know that? He might have set it up to fool around with Gabriel."

"How would he know? Gabriel had never seen him before."

"Not Gabriel, but one of the people there at the party could have passed the information to the Argentine, who decided to take advantage of the situation."

"Take advantage how? Nothing else happened."

"That's the point. If I'm right, he'll show up again, this time as a savior, offering an antidote, a magic spell that will protect Gabriel from evil omens."

"It's not for nothing that I consider you my smartest friend."

"We need brains, but we also need cunning. We need to see that policeman again."

"Fuck, Irene, you said all of that just to—"

"Calm down, girlfriend. Have another beer and think it over. Why not combine business with pleasure? After all, it's not work, or at least it's not our job . . . but it is the officer's job. Take care not to end up like your friend. Relax. Don't take things so seriously. Nobody's going to kill anybody."

"I'm not all that optimistic."

"Listen. I sometimes have to go to São Paulo on the weekends for business, and I'm going this week. Why don't you come along?"

"I've never been back to São Paulo."

"Perfect. For old time's sake. I promise that you'll come back refreshed and ready to take on Gabriel."

───※───

The beachfront streets in the Zona Sul were being battered by a strong southwesterly wind. It had stirred up the sea and filled the sky with ragged clouds. The physical changes were remarkable, but there was another transformation in the spirit of the city's inhabitants, especially palpable in the beachside neighborhoods. The southwester was a harbinger of change. The locals recognized the signal. They weren't sure what it meant specifically—it could be a sign that rain was on the way, or of a strong undertow on the beaches, or it could mean that fishermen should stay home; but it could also mean that waiters were going to be in odd moods, or that Maria was going to fight with João. Just to be on the safe side, experienced people stayed alert. Knowing that the ship was shaky, such people avoided even familiar waters.

In these conditions Dona Alzira left home on Saturday, following closely behind Gabriel. The wind made it seem cold, and luckily her son headed inland, to the part of the neighborhood protected by the skyscrapers along Flamengo Beach. She'd taken along some extra money for a cab, in case Gabriel took the bus; on foot, she wouldn't be fast enough to pop into the same bus without him noticing. And it would be tough to explain what she was doing there, since she'd been home when he left. Even in a cab, it wouldn't be easy to follow him. She'd have to be lucky to find a driver patient enough to follow a bus closely enough for her to check, at every stop, whether Gabriel had disembarked.

Since the end of lunch, she'd had her plan all laid out. There would have been a problem if her son had left immediately. But to her surprise, and almost to her disappointment, he had gone back to his room and slept for a couple of hours. When he woke, he visited the bathroom, then returned to his room and closed the door again. She knew from experience, however, that he wouldn't go back to sleep; no doubt he'd put his earphones on and was listening to music. After another hour and a half, he went back to the bathroom and took a shower. She had just about decided to write the day off when she saw, from the clothes he was wearing, that he was preparing to leave. It didn't take her much time to close the window, turn off the lights, get her coat and purse, and lock up.

By the time she reached the sidewalk, Gabriel had already walked half a block, and it was only thanks to her evening ritual that she managed to pick him out in the crowd. She tried not to lose sight of him. But as soon as he turned the corner, she did. She couldn't walk any faster; she wouldn't be able to run, if it came to that. She caught up with him again at the corner. Gabriel was walking unhurriedly, almost as if merely killing time, but it was fast for her. He'd taken a left on the Rua do Catete after reaching the end of Buarque de Macedo, where they lived. He could be walking toward the Largo do Machado subway station, she thought; she couldn't have been more surprised when, after walking two blocks, she saw him enter a McDonald's. She thought that perhaps she'd mixed him up with somebody else, but when she got to the door she was even more shocked to spot him in the part of the restaurant reserved for children's parties. He was standing in the middle of a group of kids who were shouting and running around, trying to talk to somebody. She was baffled. Was this the big Saturday and Sunday afternoon mystery? She stood in the window for a couple of minutes, waiting to see if her son was meeting someone, but then he hurried out toward the street, barely giving her time to move away. She saw him look both ways down the sidewalk for someone who seemed to have just left, someone who might have passed right in front of her nose. She hid between two cars, watching her son looking both ways so anxiously that, if his gaze had passed over her, it probably wouldn't even have registered. She got the impression that his search was over, at least for that day, and decided to go home before he did.

≈

Gabriel was full of hatred. He'd forgotten that there could sometimes be two parties in the same afternoon, and that the first could be much earlier than he'd figured. Stupid. And on that same exact day the guy had been there, practically in the next room. If that wasn't enough, there was another development: what was his mother doing hiding between two cars? What was she spying on? The only possible answer was: him. How long had she been spying on him? It was better not to let her know he'd caught her. He'd let her play her ridiculous game of hide-and-seek and see where it all was going. For now, he wanted to know if she'd been the one to come up with the idea of spying on him, and why, or if someone else had suggested it. In which case: who and why?

These thoughts didn't occur to him in an orderly fashion; they were tangled with intense emotions. They weren't even so much thoughts, exactly, as they were groups of confused ideas that lacked a clear connection. The absence created by the Argentine had now been filled by the picture of his mother hiding between the cars. One thing was certain: he didn't have just one problem, he had two. And he had to solve both of them.

He couldn't say how long he'd been standing on the sidewalk, as cluelessly as a kid whose ice cream had fallen on the ground. It had grown dark. He didn't want to go back home, at least not immediately; he wasn't sure what he would do when he encountered his mother's saintly gaze inquiring whether he was ready for dinner. His thighs ached from standing in the same position for so long. His head hurt too—not too much, but enough to give him an extra little reason to feel sorry for himself. He tried to take a step, but his feet seemed glued to the sidewalk. He tried to lift them up slowly, moving them to the front and to the sides. This time it worked. After a few moments he managed to lift his feet and take a few steps. Now it wasn't just his legs and head that hurt, but his entire body. He went back to the McDonald's and took a seat at an empty table close to the door. He got up only after a while, when an employee asked him if he felt all right.

On the street, Saturday night was getting under way.

4

For the third day in a row, once his work day was over, Gabriel started walking from Copacabana back to Flamengo, where he lived. It was far—six or seven kilometers by even the most direct route. That wasn't the route he took. His trajectory was the physical, even the graphic expression of his thoughts: not only did they occur to him in zigzags, they also sometimes compelled him to retrace his steps. As on previous days, he headed toward Flamengo not because he wanted to go home, but simply because he wanted to have a direction, even if he knew he would later reverse it.

On the first day, his mother had become desperate when he arrived home two hours late. On the second day, the clock she clung to like a crucifix read eleven-ten when he came walking down the street—not his usual side of the street—and entered with the announcement that from now on he wouldn't be returning from work at a fixed time. She didn't need to worry about his dinner—she could leave the plate there and he would stick it in the micro-wave. Dona Alzira warmed up the food and said firmly that she would continue to do so as long as it took for them to overcome the current crisis. Her gestures were deter-mined as she declared herself ready to combat evil, since she was sure of one thing: she and her son had no allies in this struggle. Even Father Crisóstomo had declined to take their side.

These days, he headed toward home only because he knew that once he was physically exhausted he would want to be somewhere he could eat and sleep. He walked as if he were simply taking a stroll. The difference was that he took no pleasure in what he was doing. It wasn't pleasure he was after, though; it was less pain. It was already dark when he started winding his way down sidewalks packed with people getting off work. Most were heading home; some, especially the men, were going to stay a little longer in Copacabana to take advantage of the bars—not the ones on the beachfront, though; it was too cold there. Gabriel didn't want to have anything to do with bars or hanging out with friends after work. One's fellow man was not one's brother, as the Christians would have it. Man was the enemy. He felt like a lone wolf, walking with his eyes to the ground, his body hunched over, his shoulders rounded. He was threatened from every side, but he himself was also a threat. At some undetermined place and time in the near future, he would kill someone. So it had been said.

Once again it occurred to him that he needed a gun. Not to kill someone, but to protect himself from whoever was trying to kill him. That was the only way he could be sure whether the prediction was correct. He wasn't a murderer, even though he'd often felt like killing people. But it had never been more than a thought; he'd never seriously considered it. With his hands in his jacket pockets, he walked close to the curb, which forced him to weave through newspaper kiosks, around trash bags, past bicycles and tricycles locked to the lampposts. He also had to avoid the people standing at the corner waiting to cross the street, but this was better than walking in the middle of the sidewalk, where he never knew if the person coming at him would go to the right or to the left.

Every once in a while he took his right hand out of his pocket. He imagined pulling out a gun and firing at someone walking toward him. He didn't go so far as to make the gesture; he just pulled his hand out and raised it to his head. In his imagination, the attacker would be hit by both the first bullet and the second even before he began to fall. Both shots would hit his throat. Naturally, for this plan to work, the assailant would have to give clear signs that he was about to attack Gabriel. Since there wasn't much room between them, he couldn't wait to see how the other guy was going to attack him. He'd have to fire as soon as the other man took his hand out of his pocket. He had a man in mind, but it could just as well be a woman. Why not? If he had no idea what motive someone would have to attack him, then it might very well be a woman. He started imagining that all the women coming toward him were also possible murderers. Even normal, everyday gestures—opening a purse, switching a bag from one hand to the other—looked suspicious. He took to crossing the street in what he imagined were moments of imminent danger. But why would the murderer approach from the front? It'd be more logical for him to attack from behind, taking him completely unawares. He tried to find quieter streets, where he could maintain a prudent distance between himself and the people walking behind him. Once he turned around and retraced his steps, to see if he could surprise his stalker. It didn't matter how much time he wasted with these pirouettes. His main object wasn't getting home—he'd get there eventually. He was trying to think about his situation, and it was best to do it on the street, away from his mother's eyes and ears.

As he was crossing the Túnel Novo, which connected Copacabana and Botafogo, the narrow pedestrian walkway was deserted. He saw a few people at the exit, at the far end of the tunnel. He thought about going back and taking a bus, but decided to forge ahead. Nothing happened. It was still quite a ways to his house. Enough time to do a lot of thinking. Especially if he didn't take the most direct route.

                                                   ~

Ever since the night before, the station had been tense. The officers had their guns out, and everyone was on edge. The reason for the tension was an anonymous phone call announcing that drug traffickers were planning to force their way into the station to free their imprisoned comrades. In his meeting with his team, Espinosa tried to defuse the atmosphere, arguing that if anybody really was going to invade the station they wouldn't call in advance; besides, it wasn't the first time they'd gotten a call like that. Nobody would try anything against the station.

Just then, another call came in from the head of the detectives of the Fifth Precinct, on the Rua Mem de Sá. With the officers focused on the impending invasion, it didn't attract a lot of attention. An employee of the Cancer Hospital had called to complain about a guy who, passing himself off as a psychic, was promising the parents of young patients "pedagogical cures by correcting trajectories." Since they knew that Espinosa was looking for information about a psychic with a foreign accent, they thought the news might interest him. The man had a Spanish accent.

Espinosa learned that the psychic and his partner had a little puppet theater which they used to entertain the children in the hospital. In truth it was a way to get to the parents. With veiled insinuations, he informed them that he could provide a "powerful complement" to the children's medical treatment. Welber was dispatched to talk to people in every hospital that treated children with terminal illnesses and find out if they ever had a puppet theater perform for the children. A preliminary, superficial investigation conducted over the phone revealed that the "Argentine" lent his "assistance" to several hospitals. He used the puppets to entertain the children and ease their pain, and he also used his performances to peddle his "trajectory corrections." If he was the same psychic who had seen Gabriel—and everything seemed to indicate he was—his audience was not only children but also naive adults. Gabriel hadn't been asked for money, but other people had. Nobody could be arrested for passing themselves off as a psychic, but when the situation involved soliciting payment in exchange for promises of a cure, it became fraud, and in that instance they could investigate him based on the telephone call. Espinosa just wanted to give the guy a little scare, let him know that the police were on to him; you rarely got a conviction when you took a case like that to court. A canny lawyer could flip the situation around, making the accused look like the victim.

Equipped with the name of the hospital Espinosa had cited and the help of the detectives from the Fifth Precinct, Welber went into the field to try to gather information that might lead them to the Argentine's address. He felt like he was doing real work this time, unlike when he was working only with Gabriel's fantasies. Trying to stop someone from extorting money from the desperate parents of sick children justified a trip downtown. If he was lucky, he might manage to find the guy over the weekend. Once he'd located him, all he would have to do was hint that he'd like to take him back to the station to clarify a few things. With a little squeezing, people like that always broke down, especially foreigners.

None of the hospital receptionists knew who had placed the complaint with the police, nor did they know the couple who gave puppet shows to children. He decided to take another tack and asked to see the hospital's director. The reaction was something less than he might have hoped. The man was very busy, seeming to have more problems than all the Rio police put together, and he was indignant when he learned that a charlatan was interfering with the children's treatment. In a moment of goodwill, he took Welber to the doctor who was the chief of the section where the puppet shows would have taken place. The doctor's contribution shed little light on Welber's problem.

"I'm sorry, Detective. I don't have anything to do with the recreation department. They're the ones who schedule activities for the kids. Find the head of activities. She works in the Office of Social Assistance. It's the next-to-last door on the right, at the end of the hall."

It wasn't the next-to-last door, or the last door, and it wasn't even in that hallway, but someone who could track down escaped criminals could find a hospital employee during her working hours.

The small office could barely contain the figure of a youngish woman who must have weighed two hundred and fifty pounds.

"This is her office."

"And can I talk to her?"

"Not today."

"May I ask why?"

"Because this isn't her shift."

"Her shift?"

"We work in shifts. Nobody could stand to do this all day long."

"Right. And how can I find Dona Sônia?"

"Is she the only one who can help you?"

"I'm not sure. Actually, I've never met her. I just want information about the magician."

"Magician? I think you've got the wrong hospital, honey."

"Sorry. I need information about the guy who does puppet shows for the kids."

"Oh. That's something else. You're looking for the Hunk?"

"What?"

"The Hunk. He looks like a movie star. Every once in a while one of the mothers asks for him. The kids and the moms are all crazy about him."

"The Hunk is his name?"

"Of course not. That's just what we call him."

"And what's his real name?"

"Nobody knows. We only know his stage name: Hidalgo."

"Hidalgo?"

"Yeah. But that's not his real name."

"And how does he get paid? He doesn't have to sign a receipt?"

"He doesn't charge."

"He works for free?"

"Here in the hospital. Other places he charges."

"And do you know where else he works?"

"No. I think he does birthday parties. Is that what you're interested in?"

"Yeah, and I'd appreciate it if you'd ask him to call me. Here's my home number."

"All right. I'll talk to Sônia. She's the one who sets things up with him."

southwesterly wind

"Ask her to call me. And thanks for your help."

Welber left the hospital convinced of one thing: Hidalgo was clever. He probably used the same technique in other hospitals. That's how he'd built his gentlemanly reputation.

~

The one-room apartment facing the air shaft was located in a building on the block facing São João Batista cemetery. It was the cheapest one they'd managed to find when they'd decided to move in together in order to work more efficiently. "It'll make it easier to rehearse and perform," Stella had said. Now that a year had gone by, she was sure that she'd made the right choice. The alliance with Hidalgo was her only real option, since she didn't want to spend the rest of her life loitering in the background of dubious theatrical productions. Hidalgo was intelligent, refined, polite, and good-looking. What more could she ask for? He didn't have any money, that was true, but surely soon—in the not-too-distant future, a future so close she could smell it—they would be rich, or at least have enough money to move somewhere less depressing. She dreamed of the Avenida Atlântica, facing the sea, but she would be content with a two-bedroom apartment (she was already thinking about having a baby) anywhere that didn't look onto the cemetery. Even though it was winter, she knew what it was like to spend the summer in that apartment, with its one window facing a wall six feet away. On hot days, the only thing to do was get in the shower and let the cold water run—when the water was working. Everything around the cemetery was better suited to the dead. And she felt completely alive.

"Honey?"

"Huh."

"I forgot to tell you. There was a message from that woman at the hospital. Somebody came by looking for you."

"Did they leave a phone number?"

"Yeah. Somebody named Welber."

"Never heard of him."

"It's in my purse."

"What's in your purse?"

"The number."

Stella, seated on the bed wearing only her panties, had cotton balls between her toes and was touching up her red nail polish. Hidalgo, holding a calculator, was taking notes and reading the business pages of the newspaper. After almost five minutes, Stella spoke again.

"How can anyone call a little baby that?"

"Which little baby?"

"That Welber."

"Do you know him?"

"Of course not, honey. I'm just wondering how a mother or father can look at a baby and call him Welber, Serafim, Bonifácio . . ."

"Huh. Is that his name?"

"Hidalgo, you're not paying any attention to what I'm saying. Once you start in with your calculator, you don't notice anything else."

"Sorry, baby. As soon as I finish I'm going to pay attention not only to what you say but to what you are."

"Not so fast—the nail polish isn't dry yet."

Stella went back to the pay phone to reply to the message she'd gotten from her answering service. Welber was an ambiguous name. It could be foreign, or it could simply be low class. She was hoping he'd turn out to be foreign. They were desperate for money. Hidalgo was eking out a little from his investments in the stock market, but sometimes prices went down so much that they were left in a state of real anxiety. She worked as a government clerk, but her salary was far from enough to cover their expenses. One big children's party could see them through the week. They'd paid their rent, but their expenses went beyond their rent and the little they ate. Hidalgo made a point of dressing nicely: an attractive appearance was essential to the good first impression needed to win a client's trust. Stella thought that Hidalgo's looks, elegance, and manners were more than enough to make such an impression.

She dialed the number and an answering machine picked up. The voice didn't seem foreign. The recorded message was too short to allow any further conclusions, but her feminine instincts told her that he was someone more interested in hiding than in communicating.

She didn't leave a message; she'd call back later. Then she'd see, from the way Welber answered, whether to take the conversation any further.

"So, babe, who was he?"

"He wasn't home. His answering machine picked up. Something about the way he sounded rubbed me the wrong way."

"What do you mean?"

"I'm not exactly sure. It was a bullying voice, but trying to sound nice and polite. I'll find out when I talk to him."

"You're very perceptive."

"Sweetheart, that's my talent. Yours is charming people. Don't forget about that guy who's looking for us on the weekend. I bet it turns out to be this Welber."

"And if it is? What difference does it make?"

"I don't know."

Stella didn't consider herself to be on the same level as Hidalgo (he was, without question, favored by the gods), but she knew that she had her strong points too. She was pretty and reasonably intelligent, but her real talent lay in her extraordinary intuition. The gift had already gotten them out of several potentially awkward situations. She described it as a kind of internal light that blinked on whenever danger loomed. It wasn't infallible, but she was right far more often than she was wrong. Hidalgo, she knew, believed only in reason, even though he passed himself off as a psychic. But he respected her intuitions, which he described as extremely accurate perceptions of aspects of reality. In the same way, his "psychic" observations amounted to nothing more than playing on weaknesses he noticed in people.

They still had until Saturday, two days, to figure out if their weekend stalker and the guy named Welber were one and the same, and if so what he wanted. Hidalgo's latest forays into clairvoyance worried her, even though they'd occasionally been financially beneficial.

Daring and prudence, in the right measure and at the right moment, had guaranteed that Hidalgo had the bare minimum income to survive, especially considering the little money he had to invest in the market. They hadn't withdrawn a cent for over a year, having resolved to reinvest everything they earned until they had enough to permit themselves regular withdrawals. He'd suffered enough reverses that he'd almost abandoned the activity, but he didn't think he could live without a little risk. He'd never overdosed. He had a degree in economics from the Federal University of Rio de Janeiro, but had never worked as an economist. Just after graduation, he'd given some classes in statistics in two private colleges not renowned for the high quality of their faculties. His job as a college professor hadn't lasted even two years, and afterward he'd dabbled in the stock market and started performing marionette and puppet shows, an art he'd learned as a child from his parents, from whom he'd inherited the dolls.

Nobody had their address. All communications came through the answering service. The theatrical performances were the only activity he'd continued after meeting Stella. They provided a small but regular income.

Stella was the result of his need for a feminine voice and a partner for his children's shows. At the same time she had become his business partner, she'd also become his personal companion.

For the first time in memory, his mother wasn't home when he arrived. On the kitchen table, there was a note in round, careful handwriting: "I went to visit a girlfriend. Your dinner is in the microwave. Just warm it up for one minute. I won't be long."

She arrived almost an hour later. Her flushed cheeks and a general physical agitation perceptible a good half hour after she returned were clear signs that she hadn't been visiting a friend. He wasn't worried about where she'd been; he considered himself lucky that she was busy with something, leaving him to continue his investigations in peace. He'd have to act alone. He couldn't count on anybody else. Even the policeman, who had seemed so cooperative at first, had not only transferred the case to a freshman detective but had focused all his attention on Irene, whom Olga had presented gift-wrapped.

"Did you get my note, son?"

"I did, Mom."

"Did you eat?"

"I did."

For the last several days, they'd exchanged only short remarks about banal household matters. It had taken a while for them to realize that they were no longer really speaking; by the time they noticed, the change had become permanent. He didn't want to worry about what might or might not be going on with his mother; she didn't seem ill, and she was more active than ever. If she needed anything, she'd tell him, as she always had. Now he had to focus on more urgent tasks.

With regards to the Argentine, he would simply carry on with his plan. He'd almost found him, had missed him by a matter of seconds. He'd try to get to the restaurants earlier. As for the gun, he didn't know how to get one. Obviously, he couldn't ask Officer Espinosa—he'd risk ruining whatever was left of their relationship. He'd found out, from conversations with coworkers, that there were gun stores downtown that sold legal hunting equipment. There was a department at the back of such stores, out of sight of regular customers, where you could get your hands on any gun you wanted. The price, obviously, included the risk the sellers took selling illegal weapons. He could use the money he had been saving to buy a new car.

He didn't know anything about guns, but he figured it would have to be a revolver, because a revolver was easier to handle than a pistol and, from what he'd heard, safer. As for the brand and the caliber, the salesman could tell him what was best. The next day, at lunchtime, he would get the money from his savings account. On Saturday morning, he would go downtown. He couldn't let his mother know under any circumstances. She would keel over from the shock. The problem was that she arranged his clothes and all his belongings. He would have to hide the gun somewhere she didn't look: behind his books; beneath his mattress; in the shoe he had on, stashed inside his sock.

———

Dona Alzira had had enough. She'd exhausted all her ideas. The only time she had come close to learning anything was the day she'd decided to follow him. Yesterday evening, she had tailed the girl he worked with, whom she took to be his accomplice in whatever it was they were doing. There wasn't much housework, and some things could be put off without Gabriel noticing. Besides, she was more worried about herself than anything else. She knew her son's schedule. It wouldn't be hard to carry out her plan.

The next day, at her son's lunch hour, Dona Alzira stood across the street from his office, hidden in a newspaper kiosk, waiting for him to come out. It was her chance to find out if he would be with Olga. She thought that was the girl's name. It was cold out, but luckily it wasn't raining. She didn't know how to act in a situation like this. She had never in her life been forced to do anything like it. She felt as if she were being followed herself, and couldn't imagine what excuses she would make if her son caught her. Twisting the strap of her purse, she kept peering inside it, as if she were carrying something precious or dangerous.

At the exact moment she had predicted, Gabriel rushed out of the building. He didn't appear to be accompanied by anybody, a fact she confirmed from how he distanced himself from everyone around him by the time he reached the corner. Two blocks farther, she was surprised to see him enter a bank rather than a restaurant. On reflection, it made sense: the next day was Friday; he was probably withdrawing money for the weekend. There was a line in front of the tellers and she stood on the sidewalk for almost half an hour, peering through the windows, taking care not to be seen. She thought it was strange that he didn't get anything to eat after he left. He went back to his building without buying so much as a sandwich. He hadn't taken lunch from home, and from what she knew of her son, he wasn't the type to go all day without eating. Maybe the company provided some kind of food. She waited to see if he would emerge again in the afternoon, but he didn't.

On her way home, she decided to return to the subway station later to see if she could follow Olga again. The day before, she had managed to identify her on her way out of the office, even though she only knew her from the pictures taken at Gabriel's birthday party. She'd have enough time later in the afternoon to take care of things at home. She prepared his dinner and left it on the table along with the note she'd used the day before; she didn't even bother to compose a new one. A half hour earlier than she'd planned, she was already waiting next to the escalator in the subway station. Since Olga didn't know her, she didn't have to worry about disguising herself; she could follow her closely. She only had to worry about the possibility that her son himself would take the subway. But from what she could figure out, he wasn't coming home via the usual route.

The girl appeared alone. Unafraid of being recognized, Dona Alzira walked next to her as they approached the platform. She was worried about not managing to get in the same car, which would complicate her scheme. She got a seat for most of the way, one of the advantages of growing older, while the girl stood up, packed in with the thick crowds. When Olga managed to find a seat, it became a little tougher to watch her, since she was situated at an uncomfortable angle to Dona Alzira. Dona Alzira wasn't quick enough to get up and follow when the girl got off at Praça Saens Peña, in Tijuca. She'd have to try another time. At least she'd learned which station it was.

The adventure repeated itself the following day, but in reverse. Instead of following Olga home, she decided to wait for her early in the morning, when she went to work. She left Flamengo, giving herself plenty of time, and took the subway to Tijuca, got off at Olga's station, and started waiting. She couldn't avoid a rush of pride when they rode to Copacabana in the same train, seated practically face-to-face. She had plenty of time to examine the girl. She wasn't beautiful, but she was attractive. She was wearing heavy clothes because of the cold, but Dona Alzira could tell she had a nice figure. Her skirt was unconscionably short, but she was wearing thick woolen socks, which offered some protection against the eyes of the men on the train, who nonetheless kept looking. Her face was hard, as if hiding distressing ideas, and she seemed to have formed some kind of inner resolve. Dona Alzira was absolutely sure that whatever she was worried about had something to do with Gabriel. She didn't know how intimate their relationship was, but she was sure that the girl was the reason for her son's illness. In any case, Olga kept herself under control.

The next day was the beginning of the weekend, when Gabriel would disappear in midafternoon and return home only at night. She didn't know if things would be as easy as they'd been last time, when all she had to do was follow him for two blocks, to the restaurant. But now she had a superior mission. She wasn't tired, defeated, or lost. She felt that her every step was guided by the Lord. She feared nothing.

The small sporting-goods store carried a few hunting weapons, along with camping equipment. Nothing remarkable—a few BB guns and small-caliber shotguns. Gabriel examined the shop windows attentively, then moved inside to look at the display cases. He found nothing that looked like a weapon for personal defense. He was the only customer that Saturday morning. In fact, he'd been waiting in a corner bar until the owner opened the store. He saw him go inside with a kid who looked like a salesman. While the owner disappeared into a door at the back of the shop, the kid put on a gray apron and came over to Gabriel.

"Are you looking for anything in particular, sir?"

"Yes. Actually, I don't think you have it, though; I don't see any in the display cases."

"What is it you need? We have other merchandise as well."

"Well, I need a gun."

"We have several. Is it for hunting?"

"Not exactly. I need something smaller. Not for hunting, for personal defense."

"A revolver?"

"Yes, but I see that you don't have any."

"We do, but you need a special license for them. We can't just sell them over the counter."

"I understand. It doesn't have to be new. It could be used."

"But even used guns require permits."

"I know, but someone told me that I could get something here. They told me to ask for Mr. Alcides."

"That's the owner. Who told you that?"

"A colleague. Nobody special."

"Wait a minute, please."

Gabriel had almost given up and left when the clerk returned with the man who had opened the store.

"Yes? You're looking for a weapon?"

"Right. I was told that you—"

"Through here, please."

They went through the door at the back of the store and entered a good-sized room that had only a display case and piles of differently sized boxes heaped on the floor. The man went behind the counter and looked pointedly at Gabriel.

"You want something for personal defense, sir?"

"That's right. Have you got anything?"

"I have pistols and revolvers, new and used. Which do you prefer?"

"I don't know. I don't have any experience with guns."

"Then perhaps you shouldn't be buying one."

"I need one."

"Well, it's up to you, but I think that a gun in inexperienced hands is worse than being unarmed."

"I'll take my chances."

"Very well. For someone who's never used a firearm, I would suggest a revolver, which is safer and easier to use. A pistol has a cartridge clip—you can't see the bullets, you have to put the first bullet in yourself, and things like that. I think a revolver is better. If you're really trying to defend yourself, I'd suggest a thirty-eight, which can take out a man even if you don't hit a vital organ. With a used weapon, you can never be sure what can go wrong. A new one is better. I've got domestic and imported."

The man unlocked and opened the cabinet behind him and took out different boxes, which he heaped upon the counter. He opened them one at a time, explaining the characteristics of each weapon, inviting Gabriel to touch them, to feel their weight. As long as it was only the gun, without any ammunition, Gabriel was surprised to feel a certain pleasure when he held the weapon, but when the man opened a box of bullets and demonstrated how to load them, it sank in that he was holding something he could use to kill someone.

He left the store with a .38 Taurus revolver and a box of bullets. When he arrived home, he got rid of the wrapping and the instruction booklet, taking care not to throw them away inside the apartment. The box of bullets was harder:

in a drawer or his coat pockets, they would be more conspicuous than if left in the box. The box was small enough to fit behind his books, on the highest shelf.

Locked in his room, he sat waiting for lunch. He would start looking for the Argentine early, to avoid another near miss.

⌐⌐⌐

After lunch, he noted a slight change in his mother's routine. It wouldn't have been noticeable if her domestic schedule hadn't ordinarily been so rigidly unalterable. He didn't pay much attention to the change, as he felt that he himself had been transformed—which, he thought, might affect his mother's mood and behavior. If there was one thing that did bother him, it was the idea that he had been seeing her, as if in extremely brief flashes, in different places and at different hours of the day. He knew it was impossible: she wasn't ubiquitous, and she wasn't even strong enough physically to run around the city as quickly as his visions would have him believe. Buying the gun had excited him so much that his perception of facts and things might well have changed. To carry out his plans, he needed to remain calm, unperturbed. A little nap might be just what he needed to regain his focus. He set his alarm for two hours later.

He didn't manage to nod off even for a minute, but simply lying down was enough to change his mood. There was no reason to carry the gun during the weekend. The

Argentine wasn't his target. Besides, attempted murders usually took place on weekdays, when everything was open and there were more people on the streets. That was how he saw it. He hid the revolver in the same place he'd hidden the bullets, behind the books on a high shelf, and got ready for his tour of fast-food restaurants. On his way out, he noticed that his mother didn't say a word. No questions, no observations: that, too, was worrisome.

That afternoon's investigation proved fruitless, as did the evening's. The same thing on Sunday. He'd lost the Argentine's track. In fact, the last near miss hadn't resulted from being on the right track. It had been pure coincidence. He'd have to count on another coincidence. The only newsworthy event of the weekend, quite an upsetting one, was that he couldn't sleep. He'd hardly slept a wink the previous two nights, which made him even more agitated and tired, and made it harder to think straight.

On Monday morning, another surprise. Olga was waiting for him at the subway station.

"Olga! Did something happen?"

"Besides the fact that you're hiding from me?"

"I'm not hiding from you. It's just that I'm really busy."

"Right. Do you want to talk on the way to work?"

"I don't know what about. Nothing's going on."

"Bullshit, Gabriel! Nothing's going on. You ask me to testify before a policeman I've never met in my life, I go, I say everything you want me to say, and then you turn away and avoid me like a rabid animal. What the hell? What do you think I am? Someone with no feelings? Fuck you."

They went down the staircase into the station. Gabriel couldn't decide whether to keep going or to go back up to the street. He didn't like confrontations, especially with women. Olga was holding him by the sleeve of his coat and looking directly into his eyes, not six inches from his face. They headed toward the street with her hanging on to his sleeve.

"Let's walk to the Largo do Machado station. We can talk on the way," Olga said.

"Fine. I just want you to know that I have nothing against you."

"So why are you avoiding me?"

"I'm not avoiding you. Well, I am, but it's for your own good."

"Damn, Gabriel. I'm not a child. I'm a grown woman, and I don't need anyone avoiding me for my own good. I know what's for my own good, damn it."

"You're jumpy."

"Jumpy? I'm not now, but I might get that way if you don't tell me why you used me and then started ignoring me. Was that it? Is that the way you are? Was I wrong about you all this time?"

"I didn't use you. I was annoyed with your friend at the meeting. She was looking at the policeman the whole time. She didn't even hear what we were saying."

"Because there was nothing to hear, Gabriel. Do you still not get that? She was very nice. If he was attracted to Irene, then it's about time you understood something very simple: men are attracted to women, especially women like Irene."

"Fine. I'm no longer worried about the officer."

"So what are you worried about? That Argentine guy? He's a joker. He doesn't deserve your attention."

"I think he does. He might not just be a joker."

"I don't know what image you've conjured up for him. First it was the clairvoyant, who you decided was an all-powerful devil; then the officer, who appeared like a redeeming god. I've been wondering what your father must be like."

"I don't have a father. He died."

"Sorry. I didn't know."

"I didn't expect you to guess."

"Did he die a long time ago?"

"Yeah. I was ten."

"What did he die of? He must have been young."

"He had a collapse . . . heart attack . . . thirty-five."

"Now I understand why you looked for Officer Espinosa. It makes sense."

They walked side by side. Olga looked at him when she spoke, but he kept his eyes to the ground and blocked out her words. He was thinking about his mother. He remembered the time he'd run out of the fast-food place right where they were now walking. He'd never quite figured that one out. He preferred to think that it had been an optical illusion.

"I'll wait for you, after work."

"Why?"

"To continue our conversation. I don't like the direction it's taking. I'm too confused."

"Nothing else is going on. I'm the one who's confused. Everything will turn out fine."

"Not the way it's going now. It's better to talk than to sit by yourself imagining things."

"All right. We can walk together. I've been walking home lately."

～

On Tuesday, Gabriel didn't show up for work.

～

On Wednesday morning, just before lunch, Espinosa got a message saying that Olga Marins, a twenty-seven-year-old white woman, had fallen under a subway train at the Praça Saens Peña station, in Tijuca.

5

The image of Olga's mutilated body flashed through his mind in black and white, even though Espinosa hadn't been to the scene. The forensic specialists had had to work fast, so as not to disrupt the city's transport system. The accident occurred at morning rush hour. Witnesses referred to the large number of passengers standing on the platform, and the pushing and shoving that greets an incoming train. The place she had fallen indicated that she was on a part of the platform where incoming trains are still moving fast. Nobody saw anything. Actually, a lot of people saw something, but she was already falling. There was disagreement on the subject of whether she cried out; some said they clearly heard her scream, while others maintained that she hadn't screamed, that it was only the sharp sound of the train braking. Some people said that the screams came from the other people on the platform, not from the woman herself. For Espinosa, this was an important point: there was no reason for her to scream if she was killing herself. By the time he heard the news, the cadaver had been taken to the Forensic Institute. The investigation would be carried out by the Nineteenth Precinct, in Tijuca.

Before allowing himself to imagine links between

Gabriel and Olga's death, he waited to read the reports collected at the scene. He also wanted to chat with the man in charge of the autopsy. Olga didn't seem to match the profile of a suicide, but he couldn't rule it out completely. Besides, it wasn't his case, and it didn't fall under his jurisdiction.

The television news was all over the subway suicide. The phone rang.

"Espinosa, it wasn't a suicide! I've known Olga since college . . . fuck, we were good friends—"

"Calm down. Just because we're hearing that from TV reporters doesn't mean it's true."

"Well, it's not true! I knew Olga better than anyone. She never would have killed herself."

"So you think it was an accident?"

"What fucking accident? You knew Olga. Did she look like someone who would accidentally stumble beneath a subway train? She was pushed, damn it. That son of a bitch shoved my friend under a train."

"Who shoved your friend under a train?"

"Gabriel. Who else?"

"That's a heavy thing to accuse someone of."

"I'm not in a courtroom, Espinosa!"

"Why do you think it was Gabriel?"

"All you have to do is look at the guy to tell he's sick."

"Sick in what way?"

"Just sick. A thirty-year-old guy who lives with his mother, what do you think he is? Normal?"

"That doesn't mean he goes around pushing people under trains."

"Not pushing people, pushing Olga. That's what matters to me."

"You don't think we'd better talk about this face-to-face?"

"Fine."

An hour later, Irene crossed the Bar Lagoa toward the back room, where there were fewer people and where Espinosa was waiting. He stood to greet her. Despite the suffering caused by her friend's death and the simple way she was dressed, Espinosa thought she looked gorgeous. They shook hands. Unlike their meeting at the station, when she'd been completely at ease, even directing the conversation, Irene now seemed somewhat uncomfortable, almost wary.

"I'm sure people have told you before that you really don't seem like a police sergeant."

"Occasionally, and I always ask them what a police sergeant really seems like."

"There's a stereotype, which may well be an exaggeration, but it doesn't apply to you."

"Assuming that's a compliment, thank you."

"You're welcome."

They sat at a table in a part of the restaurant that was safely sheltered from both noise and the famously bad-tempered waiters. They talked about their work, about a policeman's daily routine, about the risks of the profession, until Espinosa felt that it was an appropriate time to introduce the question that both of them were waiting for him to ask.

"Why are you so sure that Olga was pushed?"

"We were friends. She had no secrets from me, and I know what she was like. She was strong and quick. She'd never fall off a platform, even during rush hour. Anyway, people only push and shove once the train has already stopped, not when it's just come into the station. Olga was pushed when the train was still moving, before it got to the place on the platform where she was standing."

"Which is an argument in favor of suicide."

"Or of murder."

"All right. The accident possibility isn't the strongest one, I'll admit. She was close to the front of the platform, where the train is still moving fast. If someone shoved her with their shoulder, it would be enough to make her lose her balance and fall onto the tracks. Just because that's possible, though, doesn't mean it actually happened. But I don't know why you think it was Gabriel. They were coworkers, friends, and practically dating. They liked each other, which is why he went to her when he needed help. Why would he kill her? It doesn't make sense."

"Insanity never makes sense."

"But he's not insane."

"Really? A man who harasses a policeman to investigate a murder that hasn't happened yet—and fingers the future murderer as none other than himself—isn't insane?"

"He might be eccentric, but he's not crazy."

"Eccentric is a nice way of saying crazy. When an eccentric pushes people under a train, he becomes crazy and gets locked up in the psychiatric ward."

"We don't know very much about the case. We don't know where he was at the time of the accident. He could have been walking out of his house at the time, he could have been on another subway train, miles away from the place where Olga died—"

"Or he could have left home a little earlier than usual, taken the train in the opposite direction, gotten off at Praça Saens Peña, where he knew she boarded, and, right when the train arrived, come up from behind and given her a little push. In the confusion, he could have easily slipped away, grabbed a cab back to Catete, walked into his usual station, and taken the train to work."

"It's a nice story, but there are a few things that don't quite work. The first is that in order for him to be able to kill her, Olga would have to be standing right on the edge of the platform; the second is that she knew him, which would make it hard for him to slip up without her noticing."

"He could have tried several times. He could have gone to meet her there in order to go to work together. It'd be romantic, and make it easier for him to get her where he wanted her, on the edge of the platform."

"Without anybody noticing?"

"Have you ever been on a subway platform at rush hour?"

"All right. If we assume he acted in cold blood, which I don't, there's still the question of motive."

"As I was saying: because he's nuts."

"I can't attribute every mysterious death to the presence of crazy people in the right place at the right time."

"You don't have to use this reasoning for every death. Just this one."

"When did you see her for the last time?"

"We had dinner together last week."

"Did you speak to her on the phone?"

"Once."

"And how was she?"

"Great. But even if she hadn't been, it wouldn't have made any difference. A person who's always been normal, healthy, happy, and professionally successful doesn't just decide on a whim to throw herself under a train."

"Not all suicides are noticeably disturbed. The majority are people who seem normal but who are secretly depressed."

"That wasn't the case with her. Olga wasn't depressed."

"I'll grant that you knew your friend well enough to say that she didn't kill herself, but you don't know Gabriel well enough to justify the things you're saying about him. You only saw him once, in unusual circumstances, in a tense meeting, and he was still fine, in control of the situation. You can't just accuse him of murder, with no further ado."

"But that story he was——"

"The story he told us doesn't make him insane. There are a lot of people who are easily influenced by clairvoyants, readers, psychics. How many people do you know who go to astrologers, tarot readers, shell readers, or psychics? Are they all crazy?"

"I hope you're right. My best friend died; I promise you that it wasn't an accident or a suicide. She was murdered. It would hurt less if it turned out that her murderer was an unknown maniac rather than someone she knew, liked, and trusted, but it wouldn't bring her back. I just don't want you to forget one thing: that prediction that Gabriel would kill somebody didn't specify whether the victim would be a man or a woman."

"Have you had dinner?"

"What?"

"I was wondering if you'd eaten dinner."

"Sorry, I don't think I'm going to eat. Maybe a sandwich to go with the beer."

He ordered two sandwiches and two beers.

"Were you born in Rio?"

"That's a funny way to ask if I'm a Carioca."

"I'm sure you're a Carioca, but there are Cariocas born in Rio de Janeiro, Cariocas born in other states, even Cariocas born in other countries."

"I was born in Brasília, but I've lived in Rio since I was nine. How did you know I'm not from here?"

"I didn't. I just wanted to change the subject."

"All right. We'll talk about it later."

Espinosa was encouraged by that "later." It might refer to later that same evening, which awakened his fantasies, or it could be a few days later, which hinted at pleasures over the longer term. Both possibilities enchanted him.

Traces of art deco were still visible six decades into the Bar Lagoa's existence. Much of the history of Ipanema had unfolded within those walls. Among the people sitting there at that hour were some who were completely comfortable with the place's ambience, who knew the waiters by their names (and whose names the waiters knew); other people were there to see what fashionable people were wearing, or in hopes of glimpsing a director, an artist, a writer, that summer's it-girl, or simply to try to find that unique—yet multiple—figure, the Girl from Ipanema. Among all these people sat Espinosa and Irene, at ease in the café but not quite comfortable with each other.

"What are you thinking about?"

"Well, I usually imagine rather than think. I spend most of my time daydreaming."

"In that case, you'd be better off as a novelist than as a cop; or in advertising, where we get paid to imagine things."

"The difference is that you get to exercise your imagination, while I always get tripped up by mine."

Not counting the smile she'd greeted him with, that was the first time Irene spontaneously smiled, concentrating all the charm of the world in her face. But as enchanting as

Espinosa found her, he couldn't help noticing that there was another, invisible Irene, who scared him and seemed even more intense. What scared him most was his sense that she was hiding something. He was convinced that all women were enigmatic, but that only some of them were aware of it—and that only a few of those knew how to use that power. These were exceptional women. He suspected he had one before him now.

The meeting didn't last more than an hour. Afterward, they walked to her building together, four blocks from the restaurant, but Irene didn't invite Espinosa up for a coffee. Maybe she really hadn't wanted to do anything more than offer her informed perspective on her friend's death.

He went back to the café to get his car. The clear night offered a perfect view of the mountains surrounding the bay: on one side, the Rock of Gávea and Dois Irmãos Mountain; on the other, Corcovado with its brightly lit statue of Christ the Redeemer. Despite the beauty of the evening, something was weighing on him.

He returned home thinking about Irene, her relationship with Olga, the reasons she'd become involved in the story in the first place, and how, right after she'd come onto the scene, Olga had tragically and mysteriously died. Finally: what did she want from him?

❧

He sat down in the rocking chair in the living room, unaware of exactly where he'd parked the car or how he'd walked upstairs to his apartment. He hadn't noticed if the lights were on or off (on bad days he didn't even bother to switch them on). He let his arm droop to the side of the chair and was surprised not to feel the fur of the dog that wasn't even his yet. He collected his arm, remembering that he hadn't seen Alice for a few days. There was a dark curtain in front of him, and he realized he hadn't opened the blinds yet. He didn't get up to open them, and he didn't stretch out his hand to turn on the lamp next to him. He thought about Irene's beauty; about Alice's happy youth; about Neighbor, who was still nursing; about Olga, dead beneath the subway train. He dozed off and awoke a few times, still in the rocking chair. He moved to his bed in the middle of the night, with his body aching, his leg asleep, and a vague understanding of what was meant by the term "middle-aged."

Once again he left home late, missing Alice's company. At the station, the day's first call was from Gabriel.

"Sergeant, it's horrible, we just heard yesterday in the office. I'm shocked. I don't know what to think."

"I'm very sorry. Did she seem depressed lately?"

"No. Actually . . . she was happy."

"Did she call you before leaving home?"

"No. She didn't. She never did."

"What time did you get to work?"

"The same time as always, nine, more or less. Why are you asking me?"

"Because she might have killed herself, and anything she might have told you on the phone before she left could help us."

"What's going to happen now?"

"The Nineteenth Precinct, in Tijuca, is investigating. Olga's death happened outside our jurisdiction."

"Investigating?"

"Whenever someone dies in circumstances such as those in which she died, an investigation is opened, to see if there was any foul play."

"What do you mean? Wasn't it suicide?"

"We're not sure about that."

"Could it have been an accident?"

"Among other things."

"What other things?"

"When a person dies beneath an oncoming train, it could be the person's own fault, it could be the fault of a third party, or it could be an accident, like slipping on a banana peel. Unlikely, but not impossible."

"You're saying that it might not have been suicide? That someone might have pushed her?"

"It's a possibility."

"But who would do something like that?"

"I was going to ask you the same question. You were a friend and colleague. Do you know anyone who might have wanted to see her dead? That is, if we consider the possibility that it was the work of a third party."

"Nobody. Absolutely nobody. Really, absolutely nobody."

"In that case, we'll have to discard the possibility."

"Yes. Of course. It's absurd. Absolutely nobody. Talk to you later."

Espinosa learned some details of the autopsy over the phone, before the full report was written up. Olga wasn't drunk, hadn't taken any drugs, had eaten a normal break-fast. The examiners would account for the wounds on her body—whether they all came from the collision with the train—later.

Before an hour had gone by, Gabriel called again.

"Officer, I'm sorry to bother you again. In our previous conversation, you mentioned an investigation."

"Yes, opened by the Nineteenth Precinct."

"You mean . . . it's possible . . . it could be . . ."

"That you could be called to testify?"

"Right . . ."

"Unlikely. There's no reason for it. Or is there?"

"No, of course, but since we were talking about . . ."

"Our conversations weren't official, as we agreed. What you told me won't be repeated to the sergeant investigating the case, unless I think it's important in shedding light on your friend's death."

"Do you think it's important?"

"No, not for the time being. Do you?"

"No. Of course not. But you know better than I do what the police are like. They're suspicious of everything. They might want to connect our discussions with Olga's death."

"And is there a connection?"

"No. Of course not."

"So then there's no reason to worry about it."

"Thank you, sir. You've been very patient with me. Good-bye."

Gabriel wasn't as concerned by his friend's death as he was by the possibility of getting mixed up with the police, which didn't surprise Espinosa. The impression most people had of the police was enough to transform grief into worry, especially when faced with a murder investigation.

At the end of the afternoon, Welber arrived at the station.

"I found the Argentine," he said, rubbing his hands together in childlike glee. "I got his number from an employee at the Cancer Hospital. I called the answering service and left a message with my telephone number. Today I managed to speak to a woman who seems to be his business partner. She was really wary and kept asking me who had told me about them, who had given me their number, et cetera. I told her that I'd seen them perform at a birthday party for a son of a friend of mine, and said I'd like them to do the same for my own son's birthday. I think she was still skeptical. She said she'd talk to Hidalgo—that's the name he uses—and that she'd call me back. I've got to be careful—they might get scared off."

"Welber, the girl's death might have been an accident, but it might not have been. We'd better keep an eye out, not just for the Argentine, but also for the other elements of the group that sat in this office a few days ago."

"You don't think it was an accident?"

"A person can fall in front of an oncoming train at the exact moment the train is arriving, but that's just as rare, or rarer, than cases when they're pushed by somebody else. And there's nothing about Olga that makes her a plausible suicide, other than the fact that anyone alive could be described as such. It's time to talk to this Argentine, and in the meantime we need to keep an eye on Gabriel. It'd also be interesting to talk to his mother. We don't know what she knows about this whole thing. Think of a reason to interview her about her son—no need to scare her. Without him there, obviously. And try to find out when Gabriel got to work yesterday."

"Are we going to take over the case?"

"No, it's still with the Nineteenth Precinct. Let's focus on Gabriel. And make a date with the Argentine for your son's birthday."

Welber exited, leaving Espinosa alone in the room. For the umpteenth time, he looked at the old wooden furniture, dating to the installation of the precinct offices in the building, handed down from earlier administrations, and for the umpteenth time he wondered what any of it had to do with him. The furniture, the office supplies, the dated computer, the old typewriter (which he used more than the computer), the files, the pictures on the walls, and the traces, not always obvious, of the military regime. He thought about Irene, who lived in such a different universe.

Before he left, he called Gabriel. He thought about how long it would take him to get home, allowing a margin for possible delays. He hadn't arrived yet. On the other end of the line, an anxious female voice asked, Would you like to leave a message, sir? Yes, please, tell him that Espinosa called. You can make a note of my home number, ma'am. Ask him to call when he gets home. Thank you.

Gabriel called at ten-thirty.

"Officer, I'm sorry, I'm only now getting in. Did something happen?"

"Besides Olga's death? No, nothing."

"That's what I meant to say."

"Of course. Stay late at the office?"

"No. I've been walking home lately, and that's why I get back so late."

"You walk from Copacabana to Flamengo every day?"

"Yeah. That's what I've been doing. It's good for thinking."

"Would you like to meet up with me tomorrow, to talk about what you've been thinking about? It could be at lunchtime, like the first time we met. I don't want to interfere with your work schedule. How about noon, in the same restaurant?"

"Su . . . sure. Noon. That's fine."

"Well, see you tomorrow. Good night."

"Good night, Officer."

The morning was productive. Welber managed to set a date with the Argentine's partner for the following Sunday, in a restaurant located only a block from the station. There might even be a children's party going on at that hour, so the pair wouldn't be scared off, and that way he could get to them as soon as they came in. He didn't see any risk for the other people there. From what he'd heard at the hospital, the Argentine was friendly and polite.

≈

It was twelve-fifteen when Gabriel reached the restaurant. The first customers were arriving for lunch, and the place would soon be packed. Espinosa was already seated at a two-person table in a corner of the dining room, with only two tables next to him. It took Gabriel a minute to get oriented and spot the officer. He walked uncertainly; it seemed that he might retrace his steps and flee at a moment's notice. His clothes and hair were disheveled; he appeared to have come not from the office but from his house, and to have slept in the clothes he was wearing.

"Hello, Officer. I'm sorry I'm late; I didn't remember exactly where the restaurant was."

The voice had lost its adolescent tone, and the body seemed heavier. In a few days, Gabriel had become a man, a painful passage.

"Hello. Sit down. You look tired."

"I am. These last few days have been tiring."

"Before anything else, let's order. I haven't had lunch yet, and I guess you haven't either. There's not a lot to choose from, but the food is good."

Gabriel ended up ordering the same thing Espinosa did. Ever since he'd arrived, he'd been looking at Espinosa as if he was trying to decipher something. He looked as if he was about to start talking, but Espinosa spoke first.

"Olga's death must have really affected you."

"Until now I didn't understand what had happened. I thought it was an accident. Then I thought it was a suicide. Until you mentioned the possibility of murder. I don't understand how anybody could have pushed Olga under a train."

"I didn't say it was a murder. I just said that that was a possibility."

"Even that is hard to accept."

"You said on the phone that you've been walking home from work. It's a long way. Even for a young, healthy person like you, it must wear you out. Especially after a day at work. You also said that it's the way you've found to think. Can I ask you if you've been thinking about Olga during those walks?"

"I have been, but not in the same way. Before, I thought of her alive, with her whole life ahead of her. Then I thought of her alive, but without her whole life ahead of her. I can only think about her alive, but I know that she's dead. There's no future, and nothing to do about it."

"She was really important to you, wasn't she?"

"She was. I don't know how, but she was. I was attracted to her, but I was a little scared of her too. Not at work: she was a great colleague. But she scared me when we were alone."

"And was that often?"

"No, not really."

"Why not? She was a pretty, attractive girl. You weren't a couple?"

"I don't know. It might seem ridiculous—I'm not a teenager—but I'm not sure if we were a couple. At least in the sense of couples who are dating normally. I think we were on the verge of beginning something a few days before she died."

"And you didn't?"

"I don't think so. It's hard to explain. I don't know what happened."

"You don't have to explain anything to me. Wouldn't it be better if you just tried to tell me what happened?"

"Nothing happened. I mean, a lot happened, but not in the way we wanted."

The food and drinks had been put on the table, but they sat untouched. Neither man had made the slightest move toward them. The pause in Gabriel's story led both men to direct their eyes toward their plates. Espinosa picked up his silverware, but Gabriel looked at the food without really seeing it.

"What was it that should have happened but didn't?"

"On several occasions she said that we should meet outside the office, away from other people, to get to know each other better, more intimately. That's what she said. Until Monday, when she suggested that we leave work together. I would have rather gone home by myself, I had to think about a lot of things, but when we got off work she was waiting for me. We walked for hours, I don't know for how long, talking about our lives, our tastes, our plans, what we thought about religion, politics, art, music."

Gabriel stopped talking and sat staring at the plate. Espinosa began to think that the story had reached its end.

"And was it a good conversation? Did you enjoy being alone with her?"

"I'll admit, it was pleasant. It had been a long time since I'd talked about those things with someone. I felt better than when I walked home by myself. She asked me about my father. She was the first person to ask about him; everybody always asks about my mother."

"And what about your father? What's he like?"

"My father died."

"Now? Recently?"

"No, a long time ago, when I was a kid—from a heart attack. My mother doesn't like to talk about him; I think he had other women."

Another interruption. Gabriel began playing with his silverware. He touched the food with the tip of his fork, without lifting it to his mouth. He seemed not to realize that it was a plate of food.

"That's when she ruined everything."

"Who ruined everything?"

"Olga."

"What do you mean? What did she do?"

"We were walking in front of one of those little hotels

that only have the word 'hotel' in lights on the front; she said, Why don't we go in. I didn't understand the question at first, I even thought maybe someone she knew was staying there, but the way she put her arm through mine and looked into my eyes made me realize what she had on her mind."

"You didn't want to?"

"I did and I didn't. I didn't know what to do. She said that I didn't need to say anything. We went in, I registered at the desk, paid the fee for the night, and we went to the room. Bare bones. The double bed took up almost all the space. Olga said some things that I couldn't make out; her voice was distant. She stood in front of me, took off her jacket, shoes, dress, until she was only wearing her panties and bra. Since I didn't move, she came up close, kissed me, and helped me take off my clothes. Then she took off her bra and panties and embraced me. My legs were so tense that I couldn't move."

Gabriel kept playing with the food with his fork. He couldn't look Espinosa in the eyes. Espinosa could hardly hear what he was saying.

"She didn't notice that you were uncomfortable?"

"No, she did. I think she figured it was just shyness. When she saw that I wasn't moving, she smiled, pushed me, and we fell onto the bed. She thought it was all in fun, until she realized that I was panicking. Then she moved away, made me lie down on the bed, and sat in front of me with her legs crossed Indian style. My body's not pale or bloated—I exercise, I go to the beach—but next to her it looked like the body of a sick man. Olga was a force of nature. She had a strong body, pretty, with long legs, big, firm breasts, lots of pubic hair, and she showed it all to me without any shame. She sat there for a while in that position, looking at me without touching me. She was like a computer processing information. After a few minutes, or maybe seconds, she asked me, You don't like me as a woman? Of course I do, you're beautiful, much more than I imagined. So why are you avoiding me? I'm not avoiding you, I'm scared. Scared? Why? Are you gay? No, of course not. Then what's going on? I always thought you wanted to have sex with me and didn't say anything because you were shy. And it's true. So? Here we are. But I'm still scared. That's when she hugged me again. I felt the touch of her skin, her nipples against my chest, her hair falling onto my face, her legs wrapping around mine, her wet sex against my thigh, but mine was still soft, it seemed to be dead. Olga touched me, but I couldn't even feel it. My legs hurt from tensing my muscles so much. I started to sweat, my vision blurred. I thought I was going to die. I shot out of bed, threw on my clothes and shoes as fast as I could, she's asking what's going on, I opened the door, ran down the stairs, and kept running for several blocks. I don't know where I went or what I did. I got home early in the morning."

Espinosa had stopped eating. The voices in the restaurant, which had faded into the background when Gabriel was talking, suddenly grew louder. It was as if everyone had been listening to Gabriel's story in silence, and then they all resumed their conversations at the same time.

"Was it your first experience with a woman?"

Gabriel nodded. He seemed drained, in another world, but Espinosa knew that the moment had passed and wouldn't return with the same emotional intensity.

"Did you see Olga after that meeting?"

"No."

"Why did you miss work the next day?"

"I couldn't look at her. I thought I'd never go back to work. But the day after that was payday, and I needed to pay my bills. I went intending to get my money and quit. That's when I found out about her death. I couldn't manage any emotional response. I could only think that there wouldn't be another chance for me, at least with her."

"You say that after you left Olga in the hotel you walked around without knowing where you were going, that you only arrived home in the early morning, and that you don't remember anything."

"That's right."

"Did that ever happen before, that you'd walked without knowing where you'd been or what you'd done?"

"Not as far as I know."

"Have you had other blackouts in the past?"

"I don't think so."

"You didn't want to kill Olga after what happened?"

"I wanted to kill myself, not her."

"What did you do the next day?"

"The same thing I always do when I can: wander the streets."

"Where did you walk?"

"Downtown, though Flamengo Park, through Laranjeiras."

"Did you run into anybody you knew?"

"I wasn't paying attention to people. I might have walked by somebody I knew, but I didn't notice."

"You didn't want to follow Olga to the subway, to see how she was doing?"

"No, not at all. I wanted to be far away from her."

Espinosa felt that if he went any further, it would become obvious that he was interrogating Gabriel. He didn't like to force a catharsis into an investigation, except in cases when the conversation couldn't be resumed later. He didn't stop for moral reasons, but because he knew from experience that being too pushy could make future contact impossible. And he could imagine that there was going to be a lot of future contact ahead.

"You're not going to eat?"

"No, thanks, I've got to get back to work."

On the way back to the station, he got a message on his cell phone from a woman at the Forensic Institute. She was young and pretty; Espinosa had never quite understood what such an attractive young woman was doing spending her days with cadavers and body parts—not only doing it, but seeming to enjoy it. He called her.

"Espinosa, if you decided to throw yourself under a train, just for the hell of it, how would you do it?"

"You mean what would I wear or how would I do it?"

"I mean, would you go head first, back first, stomach first?"

"I think I see where you're going."

"That's right. I can guarantee that our friend fell onto the tracks and was hit by the train while lying on her back. I think it's unlikely that a person would throw herself under a train, from the top of a platform, onto her back. Even if only because someone who would do something like that would need to be sure that it was going to work, and it's not just difficult to jump backward, it's hard to tell if you're going to land in the right place. It's easier for a person to throw themselves off the top of a building while jumping backward; all you have to do is stand at the edge of a balcony or a window and lean back; there's no way to miss. It's more likely that the girl fell or was pushed. But I think I'm moving in on your turf."

Espinosa agreed with Irene that Olga was unlikely to have had an accident like that.

He took the longest route home, going through the Galeria Menescal to pick up some Arab food for dinner, but also to give himself time to think about what the pathologist had said. While he was waiting for his spiced meatballs, he couldn't help recalling that he and Gabriel both had the same habit of walking to think. He hoped the similarities ended there.

Approaching the square in front of his house, he noticed Alice and Petita at the door of the building.

"You're not thinking about Neighbor," she said when Espinosa leaned over to give her a kiss.

"The other neighbor is more important to me, and I haven't seen her in days."

"True. But I know how to talk, and he doesn't. You're not doing something important. He has to get used to your smell. The first smells are the ones that stay in their minds, and that's how they know their owners. You have to let him smell you more often."

"Who told you that?"

"My science teacher. She said that even people recognize each other first by smell."

"Then we're all smelling too little of each other. Tomorrow is Saturday. Let's go give Neighbor a sniff and let him sniff us too."

The three went up in the elevator together, Petita leading the way, stopping every few steps to make sure Alice and Espinosa were following her. Before they entered their respective apartments, they agreed to visit Neighbor in the morning.

⁕

Gabriel had started carrying a gun the day before. The only exception was his meeting with the sergeant. He didn't want to leave himself unnecessarily exposed. He knew he was taking a risk by carrying a gun without a license, but he figured that exposing himself undefended to an assassin was even riskier. He was sure that his mother hadn't found the gun or the box of bullets, hidden as they were behind the books on his top shelf; she would find them only in one of those annual cleanings when she took everything down and dusted each book, one at a time.

His mother had stopped asking about his comings and goings, restricting her activity to immediately useful domestic tasks; she even seemed to be taking on more of a life of her own, leaving the apartment more often and staying out longer. They didn't discuss Olga's death, since Gabriel wasn't even sure he'd ever mentioned her to his mother.

In the middle of the afternoon, he got ready for his usual tour of the fast-food circuit. It was raining and the wind was heavy, but he decided that he wouldn't risk missing the Argentine again. He put on the hooded nylon jacket he wore on rainy days. The garment made it easier to disguise the weapon, and to disguise himself.

Before he went out, he tried several times to reach the gun in the back of his pants. It didn't work. Even with the jacket open, the movement of removing the weapon from behind was slow, awkward, and obvious. He'd be gunned down before he could complete the gesture. He decided it was better to carry the gun in the side pocket of his jacket, grasping it in his hand so that it wouldn't shift around. After a few successful shots at an imaginary target, he unlocked the door to his room and left, shouting a "Bye" at his mom. There was no answer. Dona Alzira had left minutes earlier.

6

The rainy Saturday didn't improve Gabriel's state of mind. He spent the afternoon cruising the fast-food restaurants of Copacabana, checking every one that had a special room for birthday parties; no trace of the Argentine. He came home tired and wet, devoid of hope of success.

A change in his mother's attitude had made things even worse. She was still waiting for him when he arrived home, making his meals and washing his clothes, but she had gone strangely silent. She had stopped asking questions with hidden meanings, and she no longer made self-pitying comments. When they were home, each stayed in their own room, doors closed. Before, even when she was asleep, she'd leave her bedroom door open, just as she'd done when he was little and he'd sometimes wake up, scared, in the middle of the night. But then—Gabriel couldn't say exactly when—without warning or explanation, she'd started closing her door at night, just like her son did. Gabriel didn't register the change at first. As he would soon discover, his mother didn't have a problem; she had a cause, and she had focused all her energy on it. She only went through the motions of housework, without undue emotional expenditure. She had embarked on her mission with religious fervor, and it demanded all her attention and energy.

130

This evening, Gabriel went to sleep as soon as he'd finished eating the plate of food his mother had left in the oven. There was no light coming from beneath his mother's door, and he couldn't hear the television, which she usually watched with the volume at an unreasonable level (the very reason he'd started closing his door).

Sunday was just as unsuccessful. His mother spent the whole morning in church, while he spent the afternoon looking for the Argentine. They met only during lunch, which was eaten in near silence. The things they said merely served to camouflage the things they weren't saying. That was convenient but had started to make Gabriel uncomfortable.

The previous day's rain continued, not as intensely but just as persistently. The only difference between the street and the sky was the shade of gray. Espinosa and Welber had agreed to meet at the station a half hour before the meeting with the Argentine in the fast-food restaurant. There was no need for a third detective; nothing of what they'd heard about Stella or Hidalgo hinted at danger. At three twenty-five Espinosa left his apartment for the meeting, which he didn't imagine would take up much of his Sunday afternoon; even if it did, it wouldn't be a big loss, since he didn't really care for Sundays. He met Welber at the door of the station and they went straight to the restaurant, which was on the same street, one block toward the beach. Both wore hooded raincoats. At exactly four o'clock, just as they'd agreed, the couple turned the corner. She was wearing a miniskirt that, if it didn't impress the kids at the birthday party, would certainly keep the older boys entertained. Hidalgo, beneath a wide umbrella, walked as if expecting the rain to pause to let him pass. He was imposing. They were both carrying big nylon bags. Before they had a chance to open the door to the restaurant, Espinosa intercepted them.

"Mr. Hidalgo?"

Hidalgo stopped, glanced at Espinosa, then Welber, and then, with a leisurely expression, he looked to his partner, as if to inquire who these two characters were. Then he returned his gaze to Espinosa.

"Sir, and who might you be?" he asked with a light Spanish accent.

"Officer Espinosa. This is Detective Welber. He's the one who called to arrange this meeting. There's no children's party. We'd like to talk to you. Since you, sir, don't have a phone number or an address—or even a name, unless your name really is Hidalgo—this was the only way we had to speak with you."

"Are we under arrest?"

"Not at all. We only want to speak with you. It could be back at the station, which is only half a block away, or it could be here, over a soft drink."

"What's the matter?"

"Someone has filed a complaint against you for fraud in the Fifth Precinct, near the Cancer Hospital, where you do shows. But that's not what we're interested in. We'd like to talk to you about a guy named Gabriel."

"Who?"

"Gabriel. You did a psychic reading for him."

"Excuse me, Officer, but I don't know anybody named Gabriel, and I don't do shows like that. My partner and I do puppet and marionette shows, as you can see from the material we have in these bags. I work with children, not adults."

"We're aware of that. We also know that, sometimes, you involuntarily have visions about some child present at a show."

"That can happen to anybody. They're not intentional. I've never said I was psychic."

"I'm sure that's true. Except in the case of Gabriel."

"I already said, I don't know anybody named Gabriel."

"Why don't we go inside and have a seat? Detective Welber, will you be so kind as to bring us some soft drinks? Yes, you probably don't remember, sir. It was almost a year ago, at a birthday party in a restaurant not far from here. The guy's name is Gabriel. He was turning twenty-nine. You told him that before he turned thirty he would kill somebody."

"Oh. That guy. I didn't know his name was Gabriel. I'd never seen him before, and I've never seen him since. What's the problem?"

"Until now, nothing. Why did you predict that he would become a murderer?"

"I didn't say he'd become a murderer, I said he'd kill somebody. In war people kill each other, but that doesn't make them murderers. Even you gentlemen from the police might sometimes be forced to kill someone, in a shootout with criminals, for example, but that doesn't mean you're considered murderers. Gabriel could be one of those cases. But that's not the reason I did what I did. I wouldn't even call it a psychic reading; I'd call it a provocation. I never thought that it would mess him up so much that I would be approached by two police officers on a Sunday afternoon."

"Maybe your reading worked."

"This is what happened. As I said, I'd never seen the guy before. I was in a restaurant waiting for Stella, my partner, so that we could have something to eat and then go home. At the next table there was a small birthday party going on, only a few people, and I figured out that the guy at the head of the table was the birthday boy. He didn't seem very excited about the party, and of all the people there he spoke the softest, as if apologizing. Stella still hadn't arrived, so I started watching the party. Our tables were right next to each other: one of the guys in the group was practically sitting next to me. When the guy caught my eye, I asked what they were celebrating. Our colleague's birthday, the one at the head of the table. Waiter, bring a beer so our neighbor can join in. I said no thanks, I was waiting for somebody else, but congratulated the birthday boy. Next thing I knew a waiter put a glass of beer down on my table. From your neighbors, he said. I thanked them, and raised my glass to the birthday boy. He's going to be a brilliant administrator, I said. The guy I'd been talking to looked surprised. How do you know he's an administrator? he said. Obviously I didn't know; I'd said administrator because he looked like someone who would be an administrator, since it seems like most people who work in offices are administering something or the other. Our friend is clairvoyant! he shouted to his colleagues. By then, two girls had arrived and were standing next to me, waiting to have chairs brought over. The guy said: Tell our friend's fortune! As a birthday present. Come on! No skin off your back! Waiter, another beer for our friend! Just as a joke, I turned to one of the girls and said: What's your friend like? Gabriel? they said. He's a saint, he couldn't hurt a fly. I sat wondering how somebody could be so inoffensive that they wouldn't hurt a fly. So I agreed to tell his fortune. The table looked excited, shuffled their chairs so I could sit next to the guy. I started off with a few generic predictions, the kind of things you hear from gypsies, and I noticed that the guy was naive enough to believe anything I said. So I decided, as a birthday present, to shake him up a little and see if he would wake up, and I predicted that he'd kill somebody before his next birthday. Not as an accident, but deliberately. That's when Stella arrived. I got up and left. I never saw the guy again. I hope he hasn't killed anybody."

"Not yet, I hope. But his birthday is less than a month away."

"Sir, do you really think he's going to kill somebody?"

"You're the one who made the prediction, sir."

"But it was a joke—I was just pulling his leg."

"Maybe it worked. Did you know the girl you asked about Gabriel before you told his fortune?"

"I'd never seen her before."

"Neither of them?"

"Neither of them."

"Do you know a girl named Olga?"

"No. Should I?"

"I don't know. Anyway, you'll never meet her now. She's dead."

"And what does that have to do with this?"

"She was one of the girls there at the party."

"And she passed away?"

"Well, passed away is a nice way of saying hit by an oncoming train."

Hidalgo didn't say anything. Teenagers were chattering all around them. Rush hour at McDonald's. It was time to turn the tables, and Espinosa thought it was a good moment to interrupt the meeting.

"I'd like you to leave your address and telephone with Detective Welber so that in the future we won't have to go to this much trouble to get in touch with you."

Welber took down the information; they all got up, and a bunch of preteens rushed in to fill the vacated space. Once they were on the sidewalk, putting on their hoods and opening their umbrellas, Espinosa added:

"I suppose Hidalgo is your stage name?"

"You suppose wrong, Officer. It's my real name. Good-bye."

The pair walked off. During the whole meeting, which had only lasted fifteen minutes, Stella hadn't said a word, but neither had she missed a single nuance. The fine winter rain was still falling. The walk back to the Peixoto District, only three blocks away, plus the rain, was perfect for a good Sunday afternoon think.

～

The lighter traffic of cars and people allowed him to walk in relative peace, despite the wet sidewalk and the occasional puddle.

A few things intrigued Espinosa. The first was the Hidalgo couple, who didn't seem at all like the kind of people who would do children's puppet shows. His polite way of speaking, his perfect, even sophisticated use of the language, his impeccable clothes, and his elegant way of moving—he seemed destined to higher things than waving marionettes around fast-food restaurants. And Stella was a cute girl. The story Hidalgo told seemed too simple to be true, or to be entirely true.

After taking his raincoat off in the hallway, he noticed he had two messages. One was a note from Alice telling him that Neighbor had been happy with their visit and that she'd meet him the next day at the usual time; the second, on the answering machine, was from Irene, asking him to give her a call.

～

Espinosa waited for the echoes of his conversation with Hidalgo to quiet down before he rang Irene. Slowly, the image of the girl replaced the impression of the couple.

"Espinosa, thanks so much for calling."

"Did something happen?"

"No, nothing objective. Just a funny feeling . . . nerves, I think."

"What are you feeling?"

"Nothing, just a female thing, I shouldn't bore you with it. It's probably ridiculous, but I get the feeling I'm being followed. I can't identify anybody, it's just a feeling, but after what happened to Olga I'm a little antsy."

"It's understandable. You're still recovering from the shock. That's when all your ghosts come out, but in a few days they'll go back to their old haunts. In any case, you should try not to go out alone for the next few days. Not that there's anything to worry about really, but just to reassure yourself as long as you're feeling this way."

"I'm sure it's nothing, but I thought I'd better tell you."

"You did the right thing. Would you feel better telling me about it over a beer?"

"Do you always invite distressed citizens out for a beer?"

"Only when you're the citizen."

"Fine. Let's meet at the same place."

"Great. I'll be there in half an hour."

There was a silence while they decided who was going to hang up first. They hung up simultaneously.

It seemed to Espinosa that the years around forty were the most dangerous, in terms of dating. Close enough to thirty to still have romantic fantasies, close enough to fifty to have been made cynical by past mishaps. Espinosa hadn't given up on romance, but he'd long since lost his illusions; his critical consciousness had grown sharper, and he knew that he had to watch himself carefully if he wanted to hope for anything like a happy marriage. He didn't doubt the brilliance of sexual pleasure; he was, however, unsure about the combination of sexuality and marriage. And yet when he met a woman like Irene, he was bowled over by incredible, imaginary promises. Away from Irene, he was still conflicted enough to be able to consider himself rational. He'd never been a Casanova; women had always scared him as much as they attracted him. He was certain that men always lost their cool in romance. He'd have to deploy all of his wits to seduce Irene.

Such were his thoughts as he walked to the Bar Lagoa. Unlike the first night, it was raining, and the mountains around the Lagoa Rodrigo de Freitas were covered with clouds; there was no moon or stars. When he entered the restaurant, Irene was waiting for him.

"I live closer," she said, to justify her earlier arrival.

"I was here as soon as we hung up the phone, but my body took a while to catch up."

It seemed like a continuation of their first meeting. It was a different table, a different waiter, a different group of customers (on Sunday night it was usually filled with parents with small children), but there was still the odd simultaneous feeling of being both close to and far removed from Irene. She seemed to have come to the restaurant in the same clothes she'd been wearing at home, and Espinosa started to wonder whether her casual style wasn't actually anything but; it was extremely captivating.

The conversation didn't take long to get around to Olga. Not the accident, but the living Olga, Irene's college classmate and longtime friend.

"It was friendship at first sight," Irene said with a smile. "Every semester we took the same classes, sat next to each other, went out for drinks together, talked about life, boys. . . . We even lived together for almost a year, as soon as we got out of school."

"Did you ever fight about men?"

"I didn't even try; she got them all."

"But you're much prettier."

"That's what I think, too, but men were much more intrigued by her, and she was much more accommodating. Men were interested in me, but slept with her."

"Why do you think that was?"

"I'm not sure. Well, I'm not sure which was cause and which was effect, but at the time I was confused; I was scared of men and was only comfortable around women. Most of the men I was interested in turned out to be gay. Men scared me."

"Was Olga someone you were interested in?"

"In the broad sense of the term."

"What do you mean?"

"We weren't a couple; we lived together like sisters, even though I knew that wasn't quite the way it was."

"And how did she see your relationship?"

"I think she drifted away when she realized that I was on my way to being openly gay."

"And were you?"

"Absolutely."

"How did you feel?"

"Really alone. In a way, we were enough for each other. When Olga decided to move back in with her parents, I felt really lonely. I missed our conversations, cooking together, wearing each other's clothes. . . . I felt really lonely."

"And what happened after that?"

"We didn't see much of each other for a while; we needed time to let things calm down. After that, we started to see each other at least once a month, to keep in touch; we liked each other a lot. We were starting to grow closer again when she called me to talk about Gabriel."

"And do men still scare you?"

"If you want to know if I'm a lesbian, the answer is no. I like men, but that doesn't mean that men don't still scare me."

"How come?"

"For the same reason they're scared of women: because they have dicks."

Espinosa was surprised by the answer. Not by the content, which he agreed with, but because of the way she said it. It hadn't taken him long to realize that that was how Irene was: she didn't beat around the bush, but neither was she trying to shock the person she was talking to.

"I told you a little about myself," she said, "but I still don't know much about you."

"I got married when I was barely twenty years old and was separated before I reached thirty. Our marriage lasted long enough to allow my son to know life with a father and a mother, but not long enough for me to see him grow up; long before that, his mother moved to Washington, where they still live. We see each other at most once a year. It's like trying to read a book when you've only got the titles of the chapters. I've lived on my own for more than ten years. Women too: I only know the chapter titles. The most consistent women in my life are my cleaning lady and now Alice, a thirteen-year-old neighbor who's trying to convince me to get a dog in place of a partner, even though I know it's not the same thing."

"As long as you realize it."

⋙

In the subway, Gabriel could still imagine Olga in one of the cars or standing on the platform; worse, he also imagined he saw his mother there too. But he didn't want to get distracted. Olga was dead, and his mother was not a mortal threat. That left the Argentine. He started to consider the possibility of the Argentine as both persecutor and victim, but he concluded that he was more suited to the role of prophet than of executioner. He got out of the train and walked up the subway station stairs. He'd often taken that same walk with Olga at his side. When he tried to picture her on the train tracks, he saw her nude, a naked body sliced up by the wheels of the train. He would have preferred never to have seen her nude; he could no longer imagine her dressed. The office routine carried on unchanged, though the lack of Olga made the work environment less pleasant. Maybe he'd get used to it. For now, he was still half expecting her to peer over the wall of his cubicle. Perhaps with the passage of time, when somebody else appeared to take her place, that image of her would wash away completely.

There was still one other thing that was bothering him: his mother. Her world had always been restricted to the apartment and the immediate surrounding area—the church, the supermarket, the pharmacy, all within a short walking distance. He didn't quite get what she'd been up to lately, with her mysterious disappearances. In any case, he'd have to find out.

It was uncomfortable to walk with a gun. At the office, when he swiveled in his rotating chair, the jacket swiveled with him, bumping mutely against the wall. He'd been prepared for it, but that didn't mean he wasn't a little nervous. Nervousness had been in the air for the last few days; Olga's funeral was still fresh in everyone's minds.

At the end of the afternoon, he walked home from work. And, as always, his mother was waiting at the window and came to welcome him at the door.

"How nice that you've come home early. We can have dinner together."

Gabriel was sure that something was up. He was more than an hour late. It used to be that she got worried after fifteen minutes and was tearing her hair out after half an hour. Equally odd was the fact that she wasn't wearing a shawl on her shoulders, as if she'd just taken off her jacket. She warmed up the meal without complaint or direct questions. When they sat down to dinner, he noticed a fire in her eyes. She wasn't interested in eating. Her eyes were glued on Gabriel, waiting for the right moment.

"Son, I know your secret and I want to help you."

"My secret?"

"Gabriel, I'm your mother. I brought you into this world. You once were part of my body, and you're still a part of me. Your secrets are my secrets. If something is threatening you, it's also threatening me."

She spoke with religious fervor, the only fervor in her life. But now it was completely legitimate: no longer attached to an abstract object, it was focused on something so concrete that she felt it more in her gut than in her soul.

"What are you talking about, Mom?"

"I'm talking about our cause."

"What cause, Mom? What the devil has got into you?"

"There's no devil in me, but he's inside of you. Father Crisóstomo didn't want to pay attention to me. He said that you needed to get married and start a family. He's old, he doesn't have the courage to take on the forces of evil, he thinks that prayer is enough to make evil disappear. Well, the faithful have been praying since the Church of Christ was founded, and evil keeps getting stronger and stronger. You can't just pray against evil. You've got to fight it. And that's what we're going to do. Together."

She spoke with such passion that Gabriel had trouble making out everything she was saying; moreover, he had trouble grasping exactly where she was going with all this. What evil was she talking about? Did she think he was possessed by Satan? Why the reference to Father Crisóstomo?

"Mom, I'm not possessed by the devil. That doesn't exist. I'm just having a few problems, but everything is going to be fine."

"You don't have to try to calm me down. I'm not fragile and I'm not stupid, and I know what I'm talking about. Evil doesn't need to be measurable or spread fire on the wind: it can appear in all sorts of forms. I know that you're fighting it, but you haven't been able to defeat it. It's hard, it's very hard. You can't get rid of it, you think it's one thing and you think it's another, and the power of temptation is limitless."

Gabriel immediately thought of Olga inviting him into the hotel, stripping until she was totally naked, helping him take his clothes off, and then his impotence and flight. She hadn't hesitated an instant; she'd known exactly what she was doing.

"Mom—"

"You don't need to say anything, son. I just want you to

know that from now on we're in this together, your cause is our cause." She got up and cleared the table, putting the dishes in the sink without noticing that neither had eaten a bite.

"I forgot to tell you. Someone named Espinosa called. He asked you to call him back. A new friend?"

Gabriel still had his jacket on. The weight of the revolver made a bulge in his pocket, but his mother hadn't noticed. She also hadn't noticed that he hadn't shaved all weekend. Neither of them mentioned Olga's brutal death. Little comments—on the undercooked beans, the badly ironed shirt, the broken light bulb in the lamp in the living room—disappeared. Events of the last week, small and large, were placed in parentheses, in suspension.

The revolver was still weighing down his pocket. He would rest it on the table while his mother was doing the dishes.

"How did Dad die?"

Dona Alzira slowed down, moving her hands almost imperceptibly in the sink. She answered without turning her face toward him.

"A heart attack, son, I've already told you many times."

"At home or on the street?"

"At home. I've told you that as well."

"Was he asleep when he died?"

"No. In the shower."

"Was I home?"

"You were, but you didn't see your father dead. Only afterward, when he was already in his coffin."

After three days of unbroken fog, Tuesday dawned rain-
lessly. Places in the shade suffered because of a lack of sun,
but in Rio de Janeiro people need cloudy days to counter-
balance the long sequences of bright, clear days. The sun
still wasn't warm enough to dry off the sidewalks and park
benches, and the sandy soil of the little park was still wet;
mothers and nannies were careful with their children's
clothes.

Espinosa was walking unhurriedly toward the station
when he heard his name. He immediately recognized the
voice. Alice ran up to him, trying to keep her backpack on,
which was bouncing up and down as she ran. When he
leaned over to give her a kiss on the cheek, he noticed
immediately that something was wrong.

"What is it? Why do you look so sad?"

"Neighbor."

"What about him?"

"Nothing, he's fine, but my parents said I can't take care
of a dog that's not mine, that sometimes I don't even realize what I'm doing myself, so how can I take care of
another dog? Besides, I was going to have the key to your
apartment, and that would be even more of a responsibil-
ity, and I don't know . . ."

"They're right."

"Why? What difference does it make if I walk one dog
or two?"

"About the same difference it makes if you go out with

one boy or two—and I don't mean that your boyfriends bark and wag their tails."

"Espinosa, I'm serious."

"I am too. Besides, they're right about your having a key to my apartment."

They weren't walking arm in arm, as they usually did. Alice needed both her arms to gesture, and sometimes she walked backward in front of Espinosa so that she could look into his eyes while they discussed the situation. By the time they got to the station, she was about to cry.

"Let's not end the discussion here," he said. "Neighbor still hasn't been weaned; we've got plenty of time to talk it all over. Don't start your day off on a sad note. Have a good day at school."

Alice received his good-bye kiss with cheeks wet from tears. Espinosa didn't want her to suffer because of him. But he knew that by her age a human being had already accumulated enough grief for several Greek tragedies.

In his office, before he even took off his jacket, the phone rang. It was Gabriel.

"Good morning, Officer. I got your message, but I didn't get home until late last night, so I couldn't call you until now."

"Are you still walking home?"

"It does me some good."

"I've got news for you."

"Really?"

"We found the Argentine. I saw him on Sunday after-noon."

"You found him?"

"You didn't just make him up. He exists. You might have simply overstated the importance of his predictions."

"So he confirmed what he said?"

Espinosa summed up the conversation, underlining the reason that had led the Argentine to make his prediction.

"As you can see, it wasn't anything more than a joke in bad taste. If you want to, we can arrange a meeting with him to clear up the misunderstanding. . . . Gabriel, are you there? . . . Gabriel . . ."

"I don't want to talk to him. Anything—but a joke? The damage is done. A joke . . . I can't accept that. . . . Now there's nothing else I can do. . . ." He seemed shaken.

"Gabriel, where are you talking to me from?"

"Work."

"Wait for me at the entrance to your building in fifteen minutes."

The building wasn't too far from the station. He shouldn't have said fifteen minutes; he should have told him to come down right away. He reached the door before the fifteen minutes were up. Gabriel was already waiting for him.

"You don't look too good."

"I haven't been sleeping well. What did the Argentine tell you, sir?"

"We didn't talk for long. His wife was there too."

"Did he come to the station?"

"Let's talk somewhere else. There are too many people around here."

The building where Gabriel worked was on the Avenida Copacabana, not far from the Avenida Atlântica. They took the first cross street and walked toward the beach. They didn't talk on the way. As they turned onto the Avenida Atlântica, the vision of the great blue sea in front of them shocked them out of their silence. Espinosa spoke first. He told Gabriel how they'd found the Argentine by talking to the Cancer Hospital's director of children's activities, and about the strategy they'd used to lure him to the fast-food place. Then he related the conversation, leaving out a few details and emphasizing what Hidalgo had said about the prediction's being nothing more than a provocation, a bad joke. While he was listening to Espinosa, Gabriel's legs shook, and he looked around; he kept putting his right hand into his coat pocket. When Espinosa finished the story, Gabriel's eyes were red.

"Officer, what hurts me the most is that he said that it was a joke. I've spent a year in hell. Nothing makes sense to me anymore. My house, my job, my friends, my plans—everything, absolutely everything has lost its meaning for me. And now the guy says it was only a joke, a provocation? It doesn't make any difference now. The damage is done. If he wanted to provoke me, he's done it. It doesn't do me any good to say it was a joke. The joke came true."

"Why are you saying that? Did you kill someone?"

"Because he caused me real suffering. To say that it was only a joke—that doesn't make the suffering of the last year go away, and it doesn't give me back the year I've lost. When you've spent months and months, day after day, thinking about what he called his joke, the joke becomes real."

"You don't think you'd feel better if you talked to him?"

"Thanks, Officer. But as I said, the damage is done. I thank you for being so patient with me, and for trying to help me. We'd better leave it here. I've got to get back to work. There's no longer any reason for me to bother you."

Espinosa watched him walk away and vanish into the crowds. Gabriel no longer seemed to be a helpless kid, but neither had he become a real man. He'd just become an anomaly. The officer turned around to face the sea. There was a little wind and the waves were tall; there were only a few people on the sand and nobody in the water. He sat for a while looking out at the ocean.

"Provocation . . . a joke . . . People aren't toys. You'd have to be a psychopath to play with somebody else's life like that. A guy who plays with other people's souls needs to be punished. How can I be sure it was a joke? He could have said that just to get the officer off his back. A guy comes out of nowhere, makes a terrible prediction, disappears for a whole year without a trace, and then shows up well dressed, snobby, superior, saying that it was only a joke, and the officer expects me to believe it?"

"It was a disguise, son."

"A disguise of what, Mom?"

"Of the Prince of Darkness."

"Mom, there you go again."

His conversation with Espinosa had pushed him into a state of emotional suspension. He felt like someone had sucked out all his blood. Now he could think, however, without being overtaken by emotion. For the first time in several days, he'd taken public transport home. The bus. He still didn't feel quite ready for the subway. The conversation that he was having with his mother around the small kitchen table was like an uninterrupted continuation of their talk the night before.

"Your description sounds exactly like one of his disguises. He often appears as an elegant, attractive, seductive person."

"Mom, please, he's a psychopath, a pervert, not the devil."

"You can call him whatever you like, but I'm telling you he is in the service of evil, and he always appears in a misleading, captivating guise. He plays with your faith and makes you think that he's telling the truth."

"You've been talking to Father Crisóstomo too much."

"Father Crisóstomo is weak; he's got the faith of comfortable people."

Gabriel was really shaken by his mother's transformation. He'd never thought of her as weak or submissive, but she'd never revealed this side of herself, as a warrior ready to attack an enemy she herself said had a thousand faces.

He wondered if she wasn't actually in the throes of a religious delirium.

"Mom, we can't just eliminate the Argentine! He didn't do anything."

"What do you mean he didn't do anything? Can't you see that his prediction was true? You could very well kill someone before your next birthday, and that person might be you."

"I'm not planning on killing myself."

"Great. Then let's make sure that nobody else can kill you either."

They hadn't finished their dinner yet; the conversation had taken up all their energy. Both were looking at their plates as if hoping to find a solution there. They finished eating in silence, and Dona Alzira got up to do the dishes.

"Beware of woman," she said when her son started moving toward his room. "Of all of the forms Satan takes, she is the most powerful."

Gabriel didn't fall asleep immediately; he lay in bed with his room lit up by the streetlights, which shone in through the small glass windowpanes. The conversation with his mother had made him feel better than he had in a long time. He knew it would pass, that it wouldn't even last until the morning, but it still felt nice. He put his revolver under the mattress and took off his clothes to get ready for bed. That was when the image of Olga naked in the hotel room burst into his mind. He got an erection. Now it was too late. I should have gotten hard in the hotel room, with

Olga. Now there's nothing I can do about it; she's gone. She had it coming to her. He masturbated, thinking of Olga's naked body. Then he masturbated again, this time thinking of Olga's naked body spread out on the railroad tracks.

Espinosa didn't want Olga's case moved to his precinct; he would rather the Nineteenth Precinct handle the investigation. On the other hand, he knew things that his colleagues in Tijuca didn't: for them, the girl's death on the subway tracks was an isolated event, without ramifications for any other fact or person. The case hadn't awakened any media attention, and the transportation authority didn't want the news to sound sensational. Everything seemed to indicate that the girl's fall had been an accident, and the case was moving smoothly toward the files. Espinosa wasn't interested in the procedures in the Tijuca precinct; he wanted to get to the bottom of the girl's death. He didn't believe it had been an accident; suicide was even less plausible. That left murder, and Irene was the only one who believed that—she not only believed it, she claimed to know who had done it. He had to take into account the fact that the only person who claimed it had been a murder had a long-standing, close relationship with the victim, a relationship that had been broken off and was just being resumed just when Olga died. One thing, though, seemed to make sense: the series of events connecting Gabriel, Hidalgo, and Stella had nothing to do with those involving

Gabriel, Olga, and Irene. The only point of intersection was Gabriel—a fact not to be dismissed lightly.

"Welber, I want the Argentine and the woman here tomorrow, preferably before noon. Present it as an invitation; don't sound intimidating. If he declines, put it to him more persuasively."

"The girl too?"

"Absolutely. Don't be fooled by her silence; she's as much of an operator as he is. I also want you to do me a favor. It's not official. I want you to follow Gabriel when he gets off work. At least today and tomorrow. Be careful, since he knows you."

The next step in his plan was to leave a message on Irene's answering machine, the reply to which he received only that night, in his apartment.

"So, want to go out for some more beer?" Irene asked immediately.

"Unfortunately not, at least not tonight."

"Are you ever not working?"

"I don't work as much as you think. I wasn't working on the nights we went out together."

"It's just as well, because I wasn't either."

Espinosa still hadn't gotten used to Irene's responses.

"Would you be bothered if I asked you some questions over the phone?"

"I'd rather it be personally, but if I don't have a choice, then fine. What do you want to know?"

"What Olga said about Gabriel."

"Not much. She said she worked with him, that he was a nice guy, good-looking and charming, communicative, at least with her, that he was the only guy in the company she'd sleep with, but that he was really shy and had a widowed, very controlling mother; but that in spite of that she'd still go to bed with him."

"And did she?"

"I don't think so. She would have mentioned it to me."

"Was there anything between you and him?"

"Besides hate at first sight?"

"Was there?"

"He certainly hated me. I think he even fought with Olga over me."

"Why?"

"Because he hated me, I'm telling you. I don't know exactly what happened, but I think he didn't like that Olga brought me along to our meeting at the station."

"Do you know why?"

"He thought I was distracting your attention away from him. Which was true. I was sitting there thinking how ridiculous it all was."

"Did he ever say anything to you?"

"Not a word."

"What you said about him causing Olga's death—was that based on anything concrete, or was it due to emotional shock?"

"I don't have any evidence for it, but it's not baseless. Come on, Espinosa. We both know that she didn't kill herself. And we know that the possibility of an accident is highly improbable. So that leaves murder. Everybody knows somebody who at one time or another has wished that they were dead. If someone dies, all you have to do is find those people and check their alibis. In the case of Olga, Gabriel, at least, met all the conditions."

"As for the conditions, I agree with you, but there's still no motive. From what he told me, he had every reason to want her alive."

"Except frustration."

"What?"

"Because of his absolute certainty that he couldn't have her as a woman."

"Why are you saying that? Did she say something about that?"

"No. Pure feminine intuition. The only thing she said was that he was really timid sexually, that even though she'd dropped lots of hints, he'd never tried anything, not even holding her hand."

"If everyone who was shy about sex turned into a mur-derer—"

"Doesn't the saying go, People kill for two reasons, sex and money?"

"More or less."

"Well, sweetie, he doesn't have either."

"Next time, I'm taking my bike. I walked almost three hours."

"And?"

"And nothing. He's a wanderer. He seems to be heading in the general direction of his house, but he doesn't go straight there; he doesn't seem to worry if he gets there or not. Sometimes he retraces his steps for no apparent reason; he walks in circles, he crosses the street, and then crosses back to the other side for no reason; basically, the way he walks is crazy, and it takes him more than three hours to cover a distance that would take a normal person less than an hour. He didn't stop anywhere, he didn't meet anyone, he didn't call anybody on the phone, he didn't pause for water, coffee, to go to the bathroom, anything. Two things attracted my attention. One was that he rarely took his right hand out of his jacket pocket, and the few times he did, I noticed that the pocket was weighed down by something that I would bet my next paycheck was a gun. And at several points he seemed to be crying. One more thing: I could put a whole battalion behind him and he wouldn't catch on."

"Follow him again today. And don't believe that he's as out of it as all that. A guy who walks around with a gun in his pocket can't be as distracted as you think. What looks like distraction might be something else."

"And what if he is armed?"

"Don't do anything, for now. It might even be a nervous tick, and he's just holding on to something inoffensive. Another thing. The Argentine should be getting here soon. I want you to interrogate him before I talk to him.

Threaten to charge him with fraud. Don't worry if we've got proof or not—he's a foreigner and he'll get scared."

Even though nothing linked the Argentine directly to Olga's death, Espinosa thought that his prediction and her death were at least a strange coincidence. Naturally, for everything to make sense, he'd still have to determine that she had been murdered and that there was a connection between Gabriel and the murderer.

At eleven-thirty Welber came back into Espinosa's office.

"I've been with the couple for almost an hour. They're not easy. He's arrogant and won't let himself be intimidated. I think it's time for you to talk to them."

Hidalgo and Stella were in a small room whose single window was closed. The room contained a desk with no drawers and four chairs, two of which were occupied by the couple. There were two ashtrays on the table. There was also an old filing cabinet that didn't fit in any other office in the old building. When Espinosa came in, accompanied by Welber, the Argentine looked at the officer without getting up or greeting him. Espinosa resumed the questioning.

"It seems that your conversation with Detective Welber failed to shed much light on our problem."

"Officer, there are several mistakes that we ought to clear up before you take up what you call a conversation, but which is actually an interrogation. I wasn't invited here for a social event, but ordered to appear to clear up some facts that, from what I gathered from Detective Welber's words, are pretty nebulous. Moreover, I'm not a foreigner, as your assistant has said, and I'm certainly not Argentine. I am Chilean by birth and a naturalized Brazilian. Finally, I'm a university professor and I'm not going to be intimidated by the childish hints dropped by the detective."

Espinosa was about to respond when Stella started to speak. He was surprised because he'd never heard her voice, which was surprisingly incisive.

"Officer, Hidalgo is a higher being. Nothing you can do can touch him."

"We don't want to touch either one of you; to the contrary, you are the ones who are being accused of touching innocent people who have been traumatized by the suffering you caused. I would like to make something else clear, before you two go on putting on airs. What you are doing is defined as the crime of fraud, which is punishable by five years in prison in addition to a fine. Now, with your permission, we can continue the conversation. When, and if, the conversation becomes an interrogation, you will notice the difference immediately."

Espinosa knew that he had very little to press Hidalgo with, and Hidalgo knew it too; however, the officer wasn't in the least interested in his subject's philanthropic activities in hospitals. He wanted to know about his relationship with Gabriel, if there had been any contact beside the meeting in the restaurant. The encounter stretched out for another hour, during the course of which Hidalgo and Stella didn't soften their resistance one bit. Espinosa concluded that one thing was practically certain: there was nothing between Hidalgo and Gabriel beyond their encounter at the birthday party. Another thing was that despite what Stella said, Hidalgo had no psychic powers. The two were dismissed. Espinosa figured that in spite of their arrogance, he'd scared the couple enough to put a brake on any clairvoyant impulses they might feel in the future.

7

As soon as her son left for work, Dona Alzira started her search. When she'd brushed against Gabriel's jacket, she'd felt a hard, heavy object in his outer pocket. Her late husband had kept a weapon inside a canvas bag in the wardrobe, and several times she'd had to move it when she was cleaning. She could swear that Gabriel had a revolver in his pocket. She hadn't said anything at the time, because her son was starting to open up again, and she didn't want to push him away. She hadn't noticed the shape that morning. She'd have until the afternoon to go through his room. She wasn't really looking for the gun as much as a confirmation of her fear that he was up to something that could put his life in danger.

The room was small, and she knew it well; it wouldn't take her long. In less than half an hour she'd gone through all the obvious places: under the mattress, inside the drawers, and behind the clothes in his wardrobe. But she knew that he'd hidden it somewhere hard to reach, somewhere she'd have to climb up to get to, and the highest place was the bookshelves. She didn't find the revolver, but she did find the box of bullets, and nobody hides a box of ammunition behind the books on the highest shelf in his room unless he's also hiding, probably on his own person, a gun.

The last two days had been very dull for Espinosa. The newspapers were consumed with the death of a prostitute in an apartment not far from the station. The event wouldn't have elicited a single line if the body hadn't had an ice pick buried in its chest with a note that said: "To teach all the girls to do their homework." The word that circulated among the dead woman's friends was that it was a message from the person who controlled prostitution in the area—whom everybody knew to be a policeman at Espinosa's station. The papers didn't name the cop who'd ordered the hit, but they made it clear that they knew who it was and demanded a rigorous investigation.

"What are you going to do?"

"Name a commission to investigate."

"It'll be a lot of work."

"I know, but I can't cover up something like this. How was the stakeout yesterday?"

"For a while it was just like the day before, but this time he did something that took me by surprise. All of a sudden, with no warning, he signaled to a passing taxi and left me there in the street. There was no other taxi around. I don't know if he was trying to lose me or if it was just one of those weird things he does. He never looked behind him to see if he was being followed. And yet he got into the cab so fast that nobody could come after him."

"Keep following him today. Take the mornings off to

rest. I think he noticed that he was being followed. Don't forget that he's obsessed with the idea that he's going to kill someone, so he could also be thinking that somebody is trying to kill him. If it's true that he's armed, he might want to use his weapon. Don't expose yourself. I don't want you wounded again."

Nine o'clock at night. Espinosa was preparing a ham and cheese sandwich, attempting to rekindle memories of his only trip to Paris. But no matter how many different kinds of bread he tried, and no matter how many different brands of ham and cheese he auditioned, the finished product never hit the mark. It was true that he'd lost the power to compare them—he'd tried so many that he no longer exactly remembered the prototype. Wine took him back to the experience. Over the course of the evening, with the help of a few sandwiches, he drank an entire bottle, which put him to sleep so soundly that he didn't hear the phone ringing. Only in the morning did he listen to his messages and realize how much had happened the night before. The messages only identified the caller and expressed urgency. They were almost all from Welber and from a detective on duty in the Tenth Precinct, in the neighborhood of Botafogo.

While he was eating breakfast, he called Welber. It took a few tries before the phone was picked up.

"Sorry, Welber, I told you to take the morning off and I'm the first one to wake you."

"No problem. I was already up. Before you called, the phone had already rung twice."

"That was me. What happened last night?"

"We'd better talk about it in person. I'll stop by your house in an hour."

He finished his coffee. Even after he showered, shaved, and dressed, he still had time to get through nearly the whole paper before Welber arrived. The detective didn't want to come up for coffee; he said he'd rather talk on the way to the station.

"I called you several times last night because a detective from the Tenth Precinct was looking for you. It's a long story, and it starts when I was following the guy. Like the day before, I waited for him to get off work. He stuck to the same routine as the previous day, until he got to Botafogo. When he passed the subway station, he went downstairs instead of continuing on; I waited for him to reach the platform and then followed. When I made it to the platform myself, he was nowhere to be found. I searched the whole station, but there was no sign of him, and no trains had come. That's when I realized he'd tricked me again; he must have gone up the other staircase. After that, nothing, besides the fact that he'd made me look like an idiot. Around eleven at night I was getting ready for bed when the phone rang. It was from our station. The guy said that an officer from the Tenth was looking for you because there'd been a homicide and the dead guy's wife was screaming that you'd had the guy killed. It was Stella. When they'd gotten home, Hidalgo had apparently gone to open the living room window to air out the apartment and was shot in the face. The murderer was outside, in a side passage leading to the electric and gas meters. Stella said the murderer fired and then left through the little door to the street; she didn't see anything because she was so scared, with Hidalgo lying there with his face covered with blood. Because they live on the ground floor, they have bur-glar bars, but that doesn't stop anybody from shooting in. When our colleagues from the Tenth Precinct arrived, she was shouting that Officer Espinosa had done it. Of course they didn't believe her, but they wanted to talk to you to see what was going on. I didn't say anything about follow-ing Gabriel, since it wasn't official."

They walked past the station and kept going. Espinosa spoke.

"The interval between the disappearance of Gabriel in the subway and Hidalgo's death—"

"Matches perfectly. Gabriel vanished around eight. According to Stella, Hidalgo died around nine-ten. As soon as I could, I went to Gabriel's building. Mother and son were already asleep. I managed to talk to the doorman, who was still up, watching TV. He said that Gabriel had gotten home between nine-thirty and ten. He couldn't give an exact time. That's it. I still haven't talked to Gabriel or his mother; I wanted to wait and talk to you first. Should we get some coffee?"

They went into one of the few coffee shops in Copacabana that had resisted the temptation to turn itself into a luncheonette, where you could still get a cup of coffee and a buttered roll while sitting down. The weather had stabilized, promising another series of clear days.

"I was worried about the tone Stella took with the Tenth Precinct people. I don't know what she said about the interview they'd had with us, or if she said anything about Gabriel; I only know that she kept screaming that you were responsible for her partner's death. By the time I arrived, she had already finished giving her deposition."

"If she's blaming me, that means she hasn't made a link between Gabriel and the Argentine's death."

"Chilean."

"Whatever."

"You don't think it would take a lot of nerve for him to kill the guy that we all knew he hated, at the precise hour that he knows I've been following him?"

"Maybe that will be his defense: do you think I'd be stupid enough to kill the guy under those circumstances? I might as well have called the police to witness my crime. To which we could respond: And isn't that exactly what you did? And he could say: Why would I do that? Our answer: Because you could say that you couldn't kill the guy while you were being followed by Detective Welber. To which Welber could respond: Not the whole time; you vanished right when you went downstairs into the subway. I didn't disappear, he'd say, you just lost me; I got on a subway train and went home for dinner."

"Let's go to the station, fill out a search warrant, and go

to our friend's apartment in Flamengo. I don't think he's stupid enough to shoot his declared enemy in the face and then put the gun back in his bedside table."

"If he's not stupid, he might be crazy, and crazies—"

"Can also kill people."

It was ten-forty in the morning when Dona Alzira opened the door to the apartment. She recognized one of the men as the one she'd spied through the blinds the night before, talking to the night doorman on the sidewalk in front of the entrance. She hadn't managed to make out what they were saying because the window was closed.

"Dona Alzira, these gentlemen are from the police. They'd like to speak with you, ma'am."

"Good morning, Dona Alzira. I'm Officer Espinosa, from the Twelfth Precinct, and this is Detective Welber. We have a search warrant and would like to search your apartment, especially your son's room."

"But he's not home; he's at work."

"Maybe it's better that way. Don't worry, we'll be careful."

"What are you looking for?"

"A gun."

"My son doesn't have a gun. He's a peaceful person."

"In that case, our search will confirm what you are saying."

"Why are you looking for a gun? Did Gabriel do something?"

"We don't know yet."

They combed every inch of Gabriel's room, every place where a weapon could possibly be hidden. They looked for hollow places in the walls and the floor, inside and outside the wardrobe, in the light fixture, and behind every book on the shelf; they also checked every book, to see if any of them had been hollowed out. Then they searched the bathroom, the living room, the kitchen, and finally Dona Alzira's bedroom. When they took their leave, almost two hours later, they were sure that there was no firearm hidden in the apartment.

"He's not stupid or crazy," said Welber as soon as they got to the sidewalk.

"It's still possible that it's on him."

"Or that he tossed it into a garbage can on the way home."

"Go to his office and see if he's got it with him. The mother's probably already called ahead to tell him that we searched the apartment. But if he took it with him this morning and he hasn't left the office since, he still has it on him."

"And if he does?"

"Get it."

Gabriel didn't go out for lunch, and he could barely perform the most mechanical tasks after the detective finished with the search. He was on autopilot for the whole afternoon, though ideas were shooting through his brain and his internal organs seemed to be obeying multiple, contradictory commands. The unease the policeman had provoked in him seemed to spread throughout the whole workplace. Claiming that he didn't feel well, he left early. He took the first bus that came along and was home in less than twenty minutes.

"What happened, Mom?"

"That's what I want to know. What did you do to send two cops over here with a search warrant so they could turn this place upside down looking for a gun?"

Gabriel ignored the question. Taking off his jacket and walking toward his room, he asked what they were looking for and what they'd found.

"Nothing."

"Didn't you say they went over every inch of my room?"

"That's right. They took all the clothes out of the wardrobe and all the books off the shelves."

"And?"

"And nothing. I told you."

Gabriel looked questioningly at the figure framed in the doorway, then looked back at the bookshelves and ran his hand through his hair. He was clearly baffled.

"If you're worried about the box of bullets, I'd already gotten rid of it. Like I said, they didn't find anything. They left here saying they were sorry for the inconvenience."

"You what?"

"I got rid of the bullets. You think I'm a fool?"

"How did you know about them?"

"Son, you think you can do anything I don't know about?

I know you as well as any human being can know another. I know what you're going to do before you do yourself. You don't need to keep anything from me. I've been in this struggle with you since the beginning, and I'll be with you to the very end."

"Thanks, Mom."

"There's no way they'll find the bullets."

"What did you do with them?"

"I wrapped them up and put them in the freezer, with the frozen food. They looked in the freezer, but they were looking for a revolver, not bullets. We can breathe easily now. I'll go make dinner. When this is all over, we'll go to a restaurant. Even better: we'll have your birthday dinner in a restaurant. Without the fortune-teller."

Gabriel didn't comment. His mother removed some things from the refrigerator, put a teakettle on the range, and turned on the oven. His mother's movements contrasted with the immobility of her son.

"How can you guess what I'm going to do? How did you know I'd hidden the bullets on the top shelf?"

"I don't guess. I just notice when you're up to something. I might not know what it is, but I know it's something. I didn't guess that the bullets were there, I just noticed that you were hiding something from me and figured that you would hide it in your room, somewhere I'd have trouble reaching. It was easy. I didn't expect to find a box of revolver ammunition."

"That scares me."

"What, son?"

"That transparency. It's like you can see the ideas in my head."

"But that's exactly what it's like. I'm your mother. You came from inside me. For nine months, I carried you. You didn't even need to breathe; I breathed for you. Just as you lived in me, I can see inside of you."

"I'd like to know if it wasn't the same transparency that allowed the Argentine to see through me. A clairvoyant sees through people. He's not a psychic; he just sees. Some people are more transparent than others. I must be one of those."

"Nobody else can see into you. He's not your mother. He didn't give birth to you. He's just a foreign scoundrel trying to take advantage of people. Didn't he say himself that it was only a joke?"

"He was lying. He said that to protect himself."

"People don't see through one another, son. Even I can't tell what you're thinking. It just so happens that I'm your mother and I've been taking care of you for almost thirty years. We've lived together longer than I lived with your father."

Gabriel was still standing in the doorway, stiff as a statue. Only his head moved, following his mother's movements around the kitchen.

"Why didn't you say something to me when you found the box of bullets?"

"Because if you'd hidden it from me, you didn't want me to know about it; but especially because you didn't want apartment, which didn't mean that he would actually do anything to alter its state; he would just accumulate promises to himself of future accomplishments.

Alice had moved their visits to Neighbor from Saturday to Sunday. The puppy's brothers and sisters greeted them happily, but Alice and Espinosa thought that Neighbor knew why they were there.

It was a few minutes before noon when Welber called.

"I'm only calling on Saturday morning because you asked me to."

"No problem. How did it go with Gabriel?"

"He was clean. He didn't have any weapon on him, and I didn't find one in his office. I looked inside his desk drawers and inside the file cabinet. It's a clean workplace, there's nowhere to hide anything. I also looked inside the men's and women's rest rooms. Nothing. Unless some colleague hid it for him, he's clean. I checked to see if he'd left his area that morning, if he'd gone to other floors in the building. Nothing, he'd never gone past the door. And he couldn't have thrown it out of the window—it would have fallen in the middle of the street and someone would have seen him doing it. I confronted him with the fact that I'd been following him on Thursday night and noticed an object in his coat pocket, but he claimed it was a tape player. And I did see a Walkman and earphones in his room."

"And how did he explain his disappearance just before the Argentine's death?"

"That he didn't disappear, that he just went downstairs

to talk to me about it. And I think you still don't want to talk to me about it."

Gabriel was silent. During dinner, he remained thoughtful. He waited for his mother to start doing the dishes.

"Why can't I remember my father's death?"

"That happens with some people. They forget traumatic events, so it hurts less."

"You didn't forget."

"I was an adult. You were a child."

"Who discovered that he was dead?"

"That's the second time you've asked me about your father's death in the last couple of days. Why are you so interested, all of a sudden? We've already talked about it."

"I need to know these things. Who found his body?"

"I did, when I came home."

"You weren't home when he died?"

"No. I'd gone out to the supermarket."

"And was I home?"

"You were. When I left, your father was in the shower."

It took Gabriel a long time to fall asleep.

―――

Espinosa wasn't a big fan of weekends, with the exception of Saturday mornings, when he could take his time with the newspaper and savor his breakfast; he'd have two or more cups of coffee and eat twice the amount of toast he ate on weekdays. He also devoted some attention to his into the station, took off his coat, and sat and waited for the train. Since I was looking for a guy with a blue jacket, I wouldn't have noticed him in a white shirt. It's a good excuse. And he even said that if he'd known that he was being followed he would have asked me to come walk with him."

"It's true that his alibis are right on schedule—it's a very specific period of time."

"I noticed one thing: he doesn't look like a stalked animal anymore. Now he looks—not exactly happy, but relieved. That would be understandable after Hidalgo's death. But the only way he'd know that Hidalgo is dead is if he's the killer, right?"

"The papers didn't mention it. Maybe the officer in the Tenth Precinct wanted to keep things quiet for us, since Stella was shouting that I was responsible. I'll talk to him on Monday. We're also going to talk to Stella and Gabriel."

"You're going to let the people from the Tenth and Nineteenth in on Gabriel's involvement? After all, nobody else is even aware of his existence."

"I can't put it off forever. We're talking about two murders, and both of them are linked to him. It's Saturday. We've got the weekend to think it over."

⁓

While he was transporting his spaghetti from the freezer to the microwave, Espinosa worked through the theory that Gabriel had killed Hidalgo. First, he'd have to have known the other man's address, and, except for Welber and himself, nobody had this information. Second, he'd have to have known when he usually came home, to ambush him from his building's alleyway. These gaps held Espinosa back from coming completely clean with the policeman investigating Hidalgo's murder. With Olga's death, there were no gaps: he simply didn't know anything. The witnesses' accounts were so divergent that anybody could be a suspect. On the other hand, for someone disinclined to believe in coincidences as striking as those that linked Gabriel to the two deaths, Espinosa thought he was being overindulgent.

The idea of spending the weekend with Irene was frustrated by his first phone call. The message on her machine said that she wouldn't be home until Monday. His fantasies about Irene were displaced by imaginary scenes involving the murders. The only roles that never changed were those of the victims; everybody else took a turn playing the part of murderer, including Espinosa himself. They weren't logical exercises, just imaginary constructions, independent of the facts.

Without Irene, the weekend would be even less interesting.

⁂

Monday morning. This was the last time that he'd arrange to meet Gabriel outside the station. There was no longer any reason to protect him. Besides, he didn't even fully understand why he was going to the trouble. Echoes of his distant son, perhaps. Anyway, he wanted to check the guy out one last time before submitting him to official police interrogations.

As with their two other meetings, they used the lunch hour to meet halfway between their workplaces—and once again, as soon as they caught sight of each other, Espinosa started heading toward the Avenida Atlântica.

Neither spoke until they reached the beach. It wasn't the first time that the Avenida Atlântica had served as a site for confidential exchanges. Gabriel broke the silence.

"Why did you insist on meeting, sir?"

"To tell you that Hidalgo died."

Espinosa spoke the phrase while looking Gabriel in the eyes, watching for the faintest sign that the news wasn't new to him.

"He died?"

They were standing face-to-face. Gabriel took a few steps toward the closest bench. It occurred to Espinosa that the gesture could be a defensive tactic to cover up a compromising expression.

"He's dead?"

"Murdered. Shot in the face."

"Shot? Murdered? When?"

"Thursday night . . . just after Detective Welber lost you."

"So is that why you looked through my apartment and my office?"

"That's right."

"So I'm a suspect in the murder?"

"Based on what you yourself have told us, don't you think that we might have reason to suspect you?"

"The law requires guilty people."

"The Church likes the guilty. We look for criminals."

"And you think I might be a criminal, sir?"

"In every investigation, we start off considering everybody who could have possibly done it a suspect, but that doesn't mean that everybody who could have done it is likely to have done it."

"What do I have to do to remove myself from the list of possibilities?"

"Technically, you have to give me an irrefutable alibi. Nontechnically, you have to convince me that it wasn't you."

"The best thing I can say in my defense is that on the night of the crime I was being followed by your assistant. It'd be comical, even tragic, if I took a short detour from being followed to murder someone you know I hate. Besides, if I was going to kill him, why would I seek you out to talk about it?"

"At the time Hidalgo was killed, you weren't being followed. Technically, between the moment you disappeared into the subway and the hour you came home there was more than enough time for you to commit the crime. Even more if you consider how close you were to the victim's apartment."

"Officer, let's agree that it doesn't make sense."

"As I said, either you give me a watertight alibi, which you're not doing, or convince me that it wasn't you."

"I didn't like him, but that wasn't enough to kill him over. Objectively, I couldn't accuse the guy of doing anything. Why would I kill him? The prediction he made said that I was the threat, not him. And from what you told me, it was only a joke. Why would I want to kill him?"

"And Olga?"

"Olga? What does she have to do with the fortune-teller?"

"With him, nothing. She has to do with you."

"I'm also a suspect in her death? That's absurd."

"Her death was absurd."

"Olga was the only person I had a close relationship with. She was my friend, my . . ."

"Girlfriend?"

"Something like that."

"From what you told me, she thought of herself as your girlfriend. After all, the episode in the hotel could be seen as the beginning of a relationship."

"Well then. So why would I kill her?"

"The motives are very complicated. I'd rather start with the 'how.'"

"When Olga died, assuming she was taking the subway to work, I was also leaving for work. I couldn't be simultaneously in the Zona Norte and in the Zona Sul of Rio de Janeiro, and my coworkers have testified that I got to work at the usual time. It would be almost impossible for me to push Olga under the train at eight-thirty in the morning in the Tijuca subway station and be in Copacabana, inside my office, at nine. Especially not at rush hour. And especially because I couldn't use the subway, which was stopped because of the accident."

"All you had to do was come out and get a cab. You could make the trip in a half hour. It'd be tight, but it's not impossible."

"Officer, you said that I could technically prove that it wasn't me or convince you, nontechnically, that it wasn't me. If you were convinced that I'm a murderer, you wouldn't have called me to talk about it here on the sidewalk of the Avenida Atlântica, looking out at the sea."

"Maybe. Don't count on my being logical, though."

"What are you going to do with me? Are you going to call me to testify?"

"I'm not going to do anything. The investigations have been opened in the precincts where the crimes took place. It has nothing to do with me. At least for the time being."

Once again, Espinosa sat on the cement bench, looking out at the sea. He watched seagulls flying into the breaking waves, like surfers in a tube, before darting out just before the waves crashed. Their flights were so precise that the tips of their wings often touched the water. He lost himself in that vision of the green transparency of the curving waves, remembering how, as a child, he used to see schools of fish swimming there. He always hoped to spot a distracted bunch of fish, or a faster-than-usual wave, but he never saw a wave break and surprise a group of fish.

At first, Espinosa had believed that Gabriel was innocent. Maybe he was right. Maybe he still hadn't done anything; maybe he had only been asking for help; and
Espinosa, instead of helping, had just waited for things to
happen. And they had.

On his way back to the station, as he ate a double cheese-
burger with a double serving of orange juice, he called his
colleague at the Tenth Precinct. He informed him that
there had been a complaint against the Chilean and
described the meeting he'd had with him and his wife in
the fast-food restaurant, but he didn't bring up Gabriel. He
said he was perfectly willing to talk further about the case,
or to Stella, if she kept insisting that he was responsible for
her partner's death. In exchange, he learned that the police
had combed the whole area near the scene of the crime,
looking for the weapon; everything seemed to indicate that
the murderer hadn't bothered to get rid of it.

Welber returned at the end of the afternoon with the
information that the urban sanitation workers around
Hidalgo's building hadn't found any revolvers in the trash
bags they'd picked up, and they hadn't seen anything on
the street. The trash had been collected between ten and
eleven that night, right after the crime. If the murderer
had disposed of the gun by throwing it onto the street,
there was a good chance that they would have found it. By
the next morning, after daybreak, there would have been
zero chance of finding it. To make matters worse, nobody
in the area had seen anything. Even Stella couldn't say if
the murderer was a man or a woman. And the other people

who lived in the building, most of whom had had their televisions blaring at full volume, hadn't heard the shot.

No witnesses, no murder weapon . . .

For years, he'd chosen to eat out, for several reasons. He couldn't stand strangers in his apartment, he was an incompetent cook, he didn't like supermarkets, and he felt weird about producing and consuming the same product. That Monday night, he wasn't inclined to go find a restaurant, but he also didn't feel like warming up the frozen spaghetti in the microwave. Two sandwiches he'd bought on the way home and some leftover red wine would have to do for dinner. One of the disadvantages of living alone was a creeping disregard for the formalities surrounding a meal. If he had to eat by himself, he'd rather do it as simply as possible.

And those were the times when he felt his lack of a partner most keenly. It wasn't that he missed his ex-wife, or even any specific woman—he just wanted a relationship that lasted longer than a fleeting encounter. He resisted the word "marriage," but that was the one that occurred to him at times like this. And it was certainly the word that frightened him and led him to postpone until some invisible future the decision to invest in a longer-term relationship, should the possibility appear. In the last few days, he hadn't been able to think about Irene without being plagued by thoughts of his own broken marriage.

It was after ten. If she hadn't called by now, she

wouldn't be calling tonight. He knew that it was a stupid way to approach the problem. Why, instead of waiting for her to call, didn't he call himself? Why only react to her, instead of taking the initiative?

The plate with the sandwiches, the bottle of wine, and the glass were within arm's reach, as was the phone, on the table next to the rocking chair. He picked up the phone. Irene quickly answered.

"Hey, hon, I'm so glad you called—I didn't know if you go to sleep early or if I could still call you."

"How was São Paulo?"

"I had to stay longer than I'd planned. I only got back this afternoon and went straight to the office. I still haven't eaten anything. Have you?"

"I've got two smoked-ham sandwiches and a bottle of red wine here, ready to be devoured."

"If there are two sandwiches, then we can split them. I'll bring another bottle of wine."

After he hung up, Espinosa sat for a while in the rocking chair, facing the little balcony that looked out at the square, gazing at the buildings on the other side and the sandwiches and wine on the table, waiting for Irene. If necessary, they could go down to a convenience store to get anything else they needed for dinner. They didn't need to: Irene arrived not with only a bottle of wine but with enough bread, snacks, and cheeses for several dates. Espinosa went downstairs as soon as he saw the number of packages she was carrying as she emerged from her car. She looked happy, but he could tell she was nursing a worry. He didn't ask her anything while they walked upstairs; he waited until she'd put down her bags and he could take a good look at her.

"Did something happen?"

"Why do you ask?"

"Because you're not hiding it very well."

"Nothing more than usual."

"You still aren't hiding it very well."

"It's ridiculous; I've already talked to you about it."

"About your feeling that you're being followed?"

"Right."

"But there was no car behind yours."

"It's not a car. I can't say exactly how or when it happens. But I get the feeling, sometimes, that I've already seen a certain face somewhere. The worst thing is that I'm not exactly sure what face. It must be something I notice without even realizing it, but that stays in my memory. A kind of featureless face. It's an extremely unpleasant feeling. But I don't want that to ruin our date."

"Then let's break out the wine."

They didn't need much time or much wine for the hesitations of their previous meetings to give way to tentative touches, followed by longer investigations, culminating in a tangle of bodies.

8

Standing in the doorway, Dona Alzira looked at Gabriel as he sat on his bed, relating what had happened after his conversation with Officer Espinosa, three days earlier, on the sidewalk facing Copacabana Beach. As he talked, she moved closer and closer, until she was sitting down next to him.

"You don't think it's time for us to join forces? This isn't a personal fight you're involved in. It's much bigger than that. Evil doesn't attack evil, there's no need for that; it only attacks good. It's your real enemy. It so happens that good is unique and evil has multiple forms. They come at you together, from every side, directly and indirectly—attacking, sometimes so subtly that you mistake it for good. And that's the toughest form to fight: it makes you think it's good, so by the time the victim realizes what's going on it's too late to defend yourself. That's why we need to join forces."

"I can take care of myself, Mom."

"You don't know what you're defending yourself from. You didn't notice that Olga was one of the forms of evil. Now she's dead. It could have been you. And there's still this Irene, who, from what you tell me, managed to seduce the officer. There are a lot of people involved, and you can't protect yourself alone."

"I don't want you involved in this, Mom."

"I already am involved in this, simply because you are. Anything that has to do with you has to do with me. Even if you want to leave me out of it, I'm still affected by what affects you."

"I don't want to exclude you. I just don't want you to get hurt."

"Son, I bear your wounds on my own body."

It was late. Dona Alzira folded and unfolded the towel that she'd used to wipe down the dinner table. Even though the conversation was hard, neither of them was tense. They both talked softly, as if they were in church.

The conversation ended as it had begun: without warning. They simply stopped talking. Dona Alzira left without saying good night. It was as if the conversation continued in silence, each in their own room.

Seated on the bed in the same position, Gabriel rolled onto his side and fell asleep. He dreamed about his father beating on the door, crying to be let out of the bathroom.

Although he didn't have rigidly set work hours, Espinosa always left home at the same time. He wanted to establish a rhythm for everyone who worked under him. That morning was no different.

As soon as he started descending the last staircase in his building, he ran into Alice sitting on the first step, waiting for him.

"Hi. I was waiting for you."

"Morning. Haven't seen you all this week."

A passerby seeing them leave the building together would have thought he was a father taking his daughter to school.

"You've been having company."

"Have you been spying on me?"

"I don't need to spy on you. She doesn't make a secret of it."

"True. No need for that."

"She's pretty."

"I think so too."

"Are you going to marry her?"

"Slow down there—that's a big step."

"Why? She's pretty, she likes you—I mean, she must, or she wouldn't come over every night—and you must like her too, because it's the first time I've ever seen a woman come to your apartment so many times in a row. So why not get married?"

"Because that's not the way it is."

"So how is it?"

"We need more time."

"For what?"

"To get to know each other better. Besides, just because two people go out together doesn't mean they're getting married."

"But you aren't going out together, you're staying in together. Isn't that what getting married is?"

"Not necessarily, but it can be a start."

"What about Neighbor? You're not going to abandon him, are you?"

"No. He's ours, isn't he?"

"Now he'll have to be hers as well. What if she doesn't like him?"

"Sweetheart, for starters, let's call her by her name. Her name is Irene. Second, she doesn't live with me; she just comes to see me every once in a while. Besides, neither of us has mentioned getting married, much less Neighbor."

"Then it's time to talk, don't you think?"

"About what? Marriage or Neighbor?"

Espinosa admired the facility with which Alice talked about subjects that seemed so complicated to adults. The girl not only spoke in theory, she gave solid examples from the adult world and from her teenage friends. Over the next two blocks, she copiously illustrated her opinions about love and marriage, then ended the conversation in the same abrupt way she'd begun it.

"Here's your street. Bye."

Espinosa turned the corner toward the station, which was at the other end of the block, while Alice continued skipping toward school. The scene made Espinosa remember the time when he'd lived in the Fátima neighborhood downtown, before his parents had moved to Copacabana. Even after they'd settled down in the Peixoto District, he'd still walked to school. Thirty years later, he'd started doing the same thing, this time with Alice. The difference now was the point of arrival.

The week was ending in relative peace, which didn't

mean an absence of robberies, attacks, and murders; it just meant that nothing too unusual had happened. The only case that Espinosa was personally involved with was outside his jurisdiction, and he hadn't requisitioned it. He was still a participating observer, a term he used to describe his attitude to the facts that had appeared since his first meeting with Gabriel. The term was as ambiguous as his role in the case.

When Gabriel left for work, Dona Alzira was already gone. She'd prepared breakfast; all he had to do was turn on the coffeemaker. No note. He himself had been leaving earlier than usual, walking down the gray street past gray buildings. The neighborhood itself was gray. He got into the same subway train as a veritable army, even more somnolent than he was, of kids in public-school uniforms. When he arrived at the Copacabana station, he didn't head straight to work; he got on a bus to Ipanema. He had more than an hour before he had to be at work. Subtracting the time it would take to get another bus back to Copacabana, he had around forty minutes for his little early-morning investigation. He didn't usually go to Ipanema. The neighborhood's modernity intimidated him—its residents always seemed to be a decade ahead. He'd only dared to go to the beach there once. The immodesty with which the women showed their bodies paralyzed him; he found it both fascinating and horrifying.

He didn't stay long. The street, near the Praça Nossa

Senhora da Paz and two blocks from the beach, was one of the most expensive in Rio de Janeiro. It was a universe away from his little middle-class, ground-floor apartment in Flamengo. Irene lived well.

He got to his desk only five minutes late. He put his coat on the back of his chair and checked the lists of suppliers he had to see that day. Since Olga's death, the workplace environment had changed significantly. It had taken on a certain sadness. His colleagues had noted a small change in Gabriel's behavior: he'd started wearing a tie. He still wore jeans and a sport jacket, but he'd incorporated a tie into the ensemble, one of the many he'd inherited from his father. The outfit didn't look bad on him. People said it went well with the quieter, more serious manner he'd adopted since his friend's death.

The nights Espinosa spent with Irene seemed to block his access to her inner self. In bed, their skin, muscles, and smells joined with glances and words. Did corporal proximity and emotional intimacy belong to two different worlds? The body can submit to minute investigations, but the more affection is involved, the more emotional entanglements appear, until even the lover's body itself becomes mysterious. That was how Espinosa felt when the signals from Irene's body no longer seemed like a guarantee of access to her interiority. Not because his love had become less intense or focused, but precisely the contrary: because the limits between bodies and subjects had been blurred.

What bothered him most of all was the surprising fact that after a certain point the figures of Olga and Irene melded together into an indiscernible being. He felt like he was sleeping with one of two twins, without knowing which one.

He was all the more disturbed when he tried to separate them in his memory and they stubbornly stayed together as a single image. They were the same height, the same age, had the same skin color and body type, even though Irene was slimmer than Olga, who seemed stronger; but there was no question that their faces were different, not only because of the cut and color of their hair, but also because of their features. Mouth, nose, and eyes, beautiful in both women, were definitely different. Finally, it would be crazy to say they were the same just because he couldn't tell them apart or, worse, because he imagined them as one and the same. He knew how much his mind tended to wander, how he let his penchant for fantasy dominate his brain, but he also knew he wasn't crazy. At least not enough to confuse two different people, especially when one of them was dead.

After lunch, he walked to the beach. The sea was churning and restless; the waves broke violently and the wind lashed the huts on the beach. It was the southwesterly, starting to blow again.

It was windy throughout the afternoon. At night, Irene didn't come by or call. When he tried to reach her, the answering machine picked up. He fell asleep little inclined to optimism about the weekend.

The next morning, at a reasonable hour, the door-bell rang.

"Ready to go visit Neighbor?"

The southwesterly had covered the sky with gray clouds, but Alice's eyes seemed like two smiling blue lighthouses.

"Well? Did you talk to her about Neighbor?"

"I didn't see her yesterday."

"Ah."

"What does that mean, 'ah'?"

"I mean, ah, isn't that something."

"Ah."

"Now you're imitating me."

"I'll never be able to imitate you because I'll never be able to reproduce your charm."

"Now you're just adulating me."

"I like that term. Adulating. Have you been reading the books I lent you?"

"Of course. Or do you think I'd give them back to you without reading them? Some of them I don't read, it's true. I mean, I don't read them all the way through. They're boring. But most of them I read and like."

"I'll be more careful in my selection. I'll try to eliminate the boring ones. If you tell me which ones are boring, it'll make it easier."

They walked a whole block in silence.

"Did she stand you up?"

"Who? Irene?"

"Is there someone else?"

"She didn't stand me up because we didn't have anything planned."

"Here we are."

The dogs' owner greeted them with her usual cordiality. As did the mother. The trusting way Neighbor put his round, warm tummy in Espinosa's hand, sniffing around for fingers to lick, showed that he had no idea what human beings were capable of. The litter was growing fast. Soon, the pups would have to be weaned. Luckily, there were fewer puppies than teats, so everyone had guaranteed access to food. Alice, sitting on the ground while the puppies tried to jump up onto her legs, was regarded with affection by the babies' mother, who took advantage of the distraction to get up and stretch.

They were halfway home when it started to rain. It rained throughout the rest of the weekend.

It was the second weekend Irene had spent outside of Rio. The first time, her excuse—a business trip to São Paulo—hadn't sounded convincing, but Espinosa hadn't given it much thought. This time, after spending the rainy weekend home alone, he felt differently. But he didn't feel like asking for explanations, perhaps because Irene didn't owe him any.

Monday was still gray, but the rain had let up. He spent the morning dealing with paperwork. During lunch, he decided to go talk to Olga's parents, a decision he had been putting off for fear of meddling in the investigation in Tijuca. On the phone, he underlined the fact that the visit wasn't official, though he couldn't avoid mentioning that he was a policeman—moreover, the policeman with whom Olga, together with Gabriel and Irene, had met just before her death.

He didn't know exactly what he hoped to accomplish, since the case was being handled in another precinct, and since he didn't have access to the depositions gathered after the girl's death. He did have knowledge of the links between Olga and Gabriel and Gabriel and the Chilean, who had also died violently, unquestionably murdered. They agreed to meet that afternoon; the officer would pay a visit to the couple in Tijuca.

He expected to find an elderly couple and was surprised to find himself talking to two people barely older than he was. The tragedy had left its marks, and he could see that the couple's watches had stopped on the morning their daughter died.

"I'd like to make it clear that my visit is strictly un-official. The accident happened outside my jurisdiction, and I'm not investigating the circumstances in which she died."

"Then why are you interested, Officer?"

"Because I met Olga when I was investigating a case that had nothing to do with her, but in which she offered her testimony in support of a colleague from work. They came to the station for an off-the-record conversation."

"She told us about it. The guy's name is Gabriel."

"That's right. Truth be told, there wasn't a case; nothing had happened, except a fortune-teller had been scaring him. Olga only came by to testify that her colleague was in good mental health."

"I'm still not sure why you're interested in the circumstances of my daughter's death, Officer," the father said, raising his voice.

"I can imagine how much pain you are going through, and I know how hard it is to speak about the subject, but I'd like you to tell me what Olga said about Gabriel and our meeting at the station."

The father made an effort at composure. "I guess it's worse if we don't say anything, hoping that our daughter's death will be less real that way. What do you want to know?"

"What she told you."

"Not much. She said she went to the station, that you were nice, totally different from the image she had of policemen, and that it had all ended with your calming everyone down."

"Did she say who was there?"

"She said who was at the meeting."

"And?"

"What do you want to know? The names?"

"Please."

"You, the guy, her, and Irene."

"Did you already know Irene?"

"Of course, for years. We didn't think they were still friends." His voice changed from sadness to irritation.

"Honey, don't get annoyed, it doesn't matter anymore," Olga's mother said, but her voice also held a trace of anger.

"What doesn't matter anymore?" Espinosa asked.

"Everything," the mother responded. "Since it can't bring Olga back."

"Is there anything that you'd like to mention with regards to Irene?"

"Officer, we still don't understand why you're asking us these questions. Is there something about our daughter's death that we haven't heard? There's no reason for us to sit talking about her and her friends just to satisfy your curiosity."

"You're right. The truth is that I have little to say. My discomfort comes from a group of facts and persons linked to Olga's death. Two people linked to Gabriel, but who didn't know each other, have died violent deaths. One was Olga. Another was a foreigner named Hidalgo, killed by a shot to his face. I don't mean that Gabriel killed both of them—he has a solid alibi for Olga's death—but I don't believe in coincidences, especially when they involve murders."

"Are you trying to suggest that our daughter was murdered?"

"No. I am saying that the foreigner was murdered. As for your daughter, I still don't know anything. Now will you tell me what you were avoiding mentioning about her friend Irene?"

"We never thought Irene was a good person for her to hang around with."

"Why?"

"Well, Olga was always a girl with high moral principles, and Irene had somewhat advanced ideas about how a woman should behave in today's society." The father was now responding to Espinosa's questions.

"And what ideas were these?"

"Ideas about relationships between people," the mother answered, clearly defending the image of her daughter. "Officer, our daughter was raised here in Tijuca, a conservative neighborhood, with different friends than the kids in Ipanema. But that was only true when she went to school here close to home. When she went to college, we couldn't be sure who she was spending time with. I don't think I should have interfered in her social life—she was a grown-up, and there was no reason for us to keep asking her whom she was seeing, if she had a boyfriend, stuff like that. When she graduated and moved to São Paulo with Irene, we really lost any control over that kind of thing."

"She lived in São Paulo with Irene?"

"For a year. Then she came back. It seems they had a fight."

"Why did they go to São Paulo?"

"They said there were more professional opportunities there. They were probably right. But there was something I didn't like about it, and I didn't know what it was. I still don't. Now it doesn't matter."

"She never told you about the time she spent in São Paulo?"

"Very little. We only talked with her about purely functional, practical matters, nothing about herself or her relationship with Irene. Even when she got back, she didn't say anything. We were the ones who figured they'd had a fight."

"And what impression do you have of Irene?"

"None. We've never seen her."

"Never?"

"No. We got the feeling she didn't want to meet us, and that Olga didn't want us to meet her. We only found out that they were friends again when Olga told us about the meeting at the station."

Espinosa sat for a while in silence. The couple waited for him to say something. He didn't. When the silence became uncomfortable, Olga's father asked a question.

"Officer, do you think our daughter was murdered?"

"It's a remote hypothesis, very remote. Everything seems to indicate that it was a tragic accident."

"You wouldn't have come all the way up here to talk to us if there wasn't some reasonable doubt about her death."

"I promise that if I learn anything that can shed definitive light on her death, I'll come tell you personally. I ask you just one favor. Don't mention this conversation to anyone. For all intents and purposes, I was never here. You can be sure of one thing: I was deeply touched by Olga's death, and I'll do everything to figure out what happened. Thank you for seeing me."

He left his car parked in front of Olga's building and fol-

lowed the path she must have taken every day to the subway station to get to work. He descended the stairs, trying
to find the spot where she must have stood that morning,
with the crowds pressing around her, imagining the cold,
the bodies pressed against one another, the sound of the
train approaching, the warning from the loudspeakers to
stay behind the yellow line, the dry bump, the twisting of
the body in a desperate attempt to grab something or
someone, and perhaps the terrifying sight of the murderer.

He saw trains come and go, he saw the station fill and
empty. He tried to erase individual features, hoping that
the face of the murderer would appear to fill the void. It
was almost eight when he went back to get his car.

At home, he found six messages from Irene on his
machine. Practically one for every half hour he'd been
away. All were tender reminders of how much she missed
him, but not one mentioned that she'd been on a trip.

❦

It was a little after nine when Irene answered, on the
first ring.

"Sweetheart, I thought I wouldn't get to talk to you
today. Is there a problem?"

"I went to the subway station where Olga died."

"Any news? Are you officially on the case?"

"Nothing new. It's still with the Nineteenth. My investigations are extra-official; nobody knows about them."

"But why did you go to the station? Any clues?"

"None. I just wanted to see where it happened."

At the other end of the line, Irene said nothing. Espinosa could hear her breathing change, but she didn't speak.

"Sorry, I know how painful it is for you. I shouldn't be talking like this; I only met her once. I can't even say it hurts me. Maybe I'm just perplexed by the whole thing. Nothing like what her parents are going through."

"Did you see them?"

"Briefly, this afternoon."

"And what did they say? Did they make any reference to me?"

"They said that they'd never seen you. They're still shocked by their daughter's death. They don't understand anything about it. But they did agree with you on one point: that Olga wouldn't have fallen without the partici-pation—deliberate or not—of someone else."

"Maybe, now, you—"

"Participation of someone doesn't mean the participa-tion of Gabriel."

"I don't know why you want to defend that lunatic."

"Maybe because he's a lunatic."

"You're not a psychiatrist. Besides, even they can get it wrong."

"Why did you fight?"

"What?"

"What did you fight about?"

"You who?"

"You and Olga."

"Who said we had a fight?"

"Her parents."

"What else did they say?"

"That's all. Just that you lived together in São Paulo, and that after a year you had a fight and she came back to Rio."

"It's not a story I can tell you over the phone. Anyway, it has nothing to do with her death."

"Even a publicist can be wrong about that."

"Now you're being ironic."

"Which is a bad sign. Let's talk tomorrow."

"If you'd rather . . ."

He enjoyed a leisurely bath, then fixed himself a plate of lasagna and poured a glass of red wine. As he ate, he thought about the tone he had taken with Irene. There was no need to be unfriendly. After all, she'd left six affection-ate messages on his answering machine, and he'd acted like a cop. He was a cop. Maybe that was the difference. How would an advertising man, or a dentist, or a salesman react in a similar situation? Not like an inquisitor, surely. But Irene's unwillingness to discuss her relationship with Olga was indisputably disconcerting.

He was sure that Olga hadn't died accidentally. What objective change had provoked this subjective change? He couldn't quite say. He was intrigued by the question of who could have done it. No one linked to the case—he consid-ered the two deaths as part of a single case—seemed to be the kind of person who could push a girl under an oncom-ing train and fire point-blank into the face of a man who

was opening the windows in his own home. The successful execution of the first murder required a whole series
of unpredictable coincidences: the wild cards were as
important as anything a murderer could count on. The
second was a premeditated action that required foresight,
patience, calculation, use of a firearm, as well as a getaway
plan. Then again, maybe the two deaths had nothing to do
with each other, which would make the case even more
complicated.

When he lay down to sleep, he was still reviewing the
possibilities in his head. He continued to do so for several
hours. It was true: he was a cop, not an advertising execu-
tive, dentist, or salesman.

He felt especially uncomfortable being the only person
who knew that the deaths were connected. He was the only
one who knew of Gabriel's existence. He and Welber—but
his assistant had behaved quietly and extra-officially when
trying to locate the fortune-teller. Without knowing about
Gabriel, the investigating detectives at two different
precincts wouldn't have any idea that the two deaths could
possibly be linked. And the irony of the story was that he, a
policeman, was standing in the way of the police.

These reflections accompanied his breakfast. He'd gotten up early and intentionally prolonged his meal, adding
another cup of coffee and a few more pieces of toast with
orange marmalade, his favorite. He enjoyed moments like
this; they set the tone for the day. But such moments could

only be experienced alone. (That was one of the main reasons he didn't have a full-time maid; he preferred his cleaning lady, whom he paid by the hour and who arrived after he was already gone and left before he returned.) He enjoyed watching the light that came in through the French windows and filled up the whole living room. Breakfast and reading the paper took almost an hour, enough time to prepare his soul to face the police station. He heard a door slam and the sound of Alice running down the stairs. He could have picked up his pace in order to catch up with her, but this morning he needed to be alone, even more than usual.

He didn't think of himself as a prejudiced person, but he was fully aware that some of his values were out-of-date. He wasn't sure, for example, how he would react if he learned that the girl he was dating had had sexual relations with another woman. He wasn't sure if Irene actually had, but he was trying to brace himself for any such revelation. He didn't have any doubts about how intense her relationship with Olga had been. He knew little or nothing about Irene's life. Her weekend business trips could also be the cover for another relationship like the one she'd had with Olga, also in São Paulo. Maybe he really was prejudiced—maybe certain values had changed faster than his ability to reformulate his own. For now, though, he was getting ahead of himself. There were still many parts of Irene waiting to be discovered. He got dressed to go out.

"Officer Espinosa?" He didn't immediately recognize the diminutive figure, carrying a supermarket bag and a purse, who appeared to be waiting for him on the sidewalk in front of his building.

"Yes?"

"Sir, don't you remember me? I'm Gabriel's mother. You were at my house."

Espinosa was mortified not to recognize the woman whose house he had turned upside down. He had always been considered an excellent observer and was famous in the department for being able to describe a scene, an event, or a face with perfect accuracy. It was incomprehensible that he wouldn't recognize a person he'd met so recently and in circumstances so favorable to recollection.

"Sorry, Dona Alzira, I was just walking out the door, a little distracted, and I didn't expect to see you here in front of my building, so far from your home."

"I'm the one who should apologize for showing up out of the blue like this, but I needed to speak with you, sir."

"Should we go find a bench over in the square?"

They crossed the street and headed toward the square, which at that hour was occupied by preschool-age children and baby carriages pushed by mothers or uniformed nannies. They found a bench under an almond tree.

"What would you like to ask me about, Dona Alzira?"

"Well, it wasn't so much to ask you something, sir, but to give you this bag. I think it's what you were looking for."

When he took the bag, Espinosa immediately guessed what it was. The feel was very familiar to him.

"There's also this," she said, and she took a box of ammunition from her purse. "I was terrified when I realized that Gabriel was carrying a revolver around. It was my husband's. Since he died, it's been in the bottom of my wardrobe, wrapped up in this same towel, though I took care to throw out the bullets, because when Gabriel was a child I was afraid that he would find it. Then after he told me about the fortune-teller, and as his birthday approached, he started getting so nervous. I no longer recognized the quiet boy I'd always known. He was always so averse to violence. When I realized that he was armed, I was terrified. I asked him what was going on, and he said the gun was for self-defense, that he wasn't going to attack anybody. When I told him that the revolver didn't have any ammunition, he said he'd bought some. I was scared about what might happen, so I took the gun and the bullets and hid them at a friend's house. When you and that detective came to look through the apartment, I'd already taken the gun away. It's in the bag, wrapped up in a towel. The only thing I did was take out the bullets and put them back in the box. Before you ask me: my husband taught me how to use the gun. He said that ignorance is more dangerous than fear."

Espinosa unwrapped the gun to check the caliber. It was a Smith & Wesson .38, apparently in good condition. The box of bullets was new, of domestic manufacture, and appeared to be full.

"When did you take the revolver, ma'am?"

"A few days before you came to the apartment."

"What did Gabriel say when he found that you'd taken his gun away?"

"He said that it was the best thing. That whatever would happen, would happen."

"Thank you for bringing me this, Dona Alzira. I too was worried that your son would do something crazy."

"And I thank you for being so patient with him, Officer."

"One question. If you already had the gun when we came to your apartment, why didn't you tell me all this at the time?"

"Because I still didn't know what it was all about. I wouldn't do anything to incriminate him."

"One more thing, Dona Alzira. How did your husband die?"

"He had a heart attack. Why do you ask, sir?"

"Did Gabriel see his father die?"

"Not directly. He was home, but he didn't see his father die. Nobody did. He was in the shower when he had his attack. The help got there too late."

"How did you know he was dead?"

"It took him so long in the bathroom. I had gone out to buy some things and left my husband to bathe. I know he was fine, because he usually left the door open—he was scared of gas—and I said good-bye, telling him I'd be back in a few minutes. When I came back, the bathroom door was closed. I called him, but he didn't answer. When I opened the door and pulled back the curtain I saw him lying there in the tub, with the water overflowing."

"Why would he have closed the door?"

"I don't know. He never would have done that to take a bath."

"Did Gabriel see his father dead in the tub?"

"I can't say. But I don't think so."

"How old was your husband?"

"Thirty-five. It was just before Gabriel's tenth birthday. Why are you asking me, sir?"

"Because Gabriel brought it up. Sorry to make you talk about such a painful event."

"It's been a long time."

"In any case, thank you."

"Goodbye, Officer, and thanks once again for helping my son."

As she walked off, Espinosa noted that she was much younger than he'd previously thought. She wasn't even sixty.

From the Peixoto District, Espinosa headed straight downtown to the Forensic Institute, carrying a bag with the weapon and ammunition. He knew that the projectile extracted from the Chilean's body wouldn't yet have been sent to the officer conducting the investigation, and he knew that they needed a crime weapon to conduct any ballistics tests. Evandro, who had joined the force at the same time Espinosa had and acted as a kind of director of the Forensic Institute, was on top of everything that went on there. He was taking night classes in psychology. After examining bodies for so long, he now wanted to examine souls.

"Espinosa, great to see you. We ought to see each other

more often, even when it's not over a cadaver. But you didn't come all the way from Copacabana just to see me."

"You're right on both counts."

"What can I do for you?"

"I wanted to borrow the bullet taken from the head of the foreigner who died in Botafogo, for a ballistics exam. Off the record. I'll give it back to you today. If you want, you can come with me."

"No problem; I trust you."

The projectile was in a clear plastic envelope stapled to the autopsy report.

"Ask for Freire in ballistics. Tell him I sent you."

Espinosa thanked him and said good-bye without further ado. After twenty years on the police force, he knew everybody he could count on in every department. He'd known Freire for years, but he didn't want to cheapen Evandro's kindness by saying so. He walked over to the Carlos Éboli Institute of Criminology, which was located in the same group of buildings as the Forensic Institute. The two buildings were linked by an internal courtyard.

He'd often asked Freire for his help in difficult cases, and Freire had always done his best. A man of few words, Freire was completely professional, mistrustful of anything but solid evidence, and difficult to distract.

"I could do a comparative test right now," he said as soon as Espinosa explained what he wanted. "But I'd rather examine the weapon before testing it in the firing box. Call back this afternoon, and I'll have something to tell you."

As he did every time he visited the Forensic Institute,

Espinosa left on foot, walking down the Rua Mem de Sá toward the arches of the aqueduct at Lapa, the part of Rio that felt the most traditional. He knew these streets well; he'd lived here as a child. Before the family moved to Peixoto, they'd lived in Fátima—which, like the Peixoto District, wasn't so much a neighborhood as a group of streets. This route was part of his former walk to the Colégio Pedro II, his school. He enjoyed looking at the beautiful colonial houses and the grand arches of the Lapa aqueduct: it was a reward he allowed himself every time he had to face the brutality of death at the Forensic Institute. Before he left, he stopped to watch the little tram to Santa Teresa crossing the arches from one end to another.

He didn't have to wait till the end of the afternoon. When he got back from lunch, there was a message from Freire. He called back, and as soon as Freire picked up, the ballistics expert said, "Espinosa, there's no need to do a test. That gun hasn't been fired in at least ten years. In any case, I tested it in the firing range. Nothing. I'm absolutely sure that the bullet you brought me didn't come out of that gun. You can pick up the material today, if you want. I'll be here till five."

Espinosa returned to the Criminology Institute long before five and entered the office where Freire was working, a cross between museum, lab, and warehouse.

"I examined the barrel before I did the ballistics exam, and I checked the surface of the metal inside. Based on my experience, I'd say that nothing has been fired from that gun in years. The metal's been rusting for a long time—I can't say how long without laboratory examinations, but even including a large margin of error, I guarantee at least five years. I'd be comfortable doubling it, but I don't know if that's relevant to you. I tested it just in case, since you might need something official. The bullet you brought me didn't come from that barrel, I'm absolutely sure."

"Thanks, Freire. If I need anything in writing, I'll call you. But I don't think it'll be necessary. As always, if I can be of assistance, you know where to find me."

Espinosa left the Criminology Institute and went to the Forensic Institute to return the plastic envelope with the bullet he'd had analyzed. He went back to the station carrying the supermarket bag with Dona Alzira's wrapped-up revolver.

He felt less guilty now about withholding Gabriel's name from the officer investigating the Chilean's death; he would have been the ideal candidate for a crucifixion, due to the complete lack of other suspects. His natural fragility certainly would not have inspired any protective instincts in his inquisitors; to the contrary, it would have been the first thing they'd use against him.

Back at the station, he locked up the gun and the bullets and checked his messages. One was from Irene. The relief he'd felt from the results of Freire's exam had made the prospect of seeing her seem more promising. She herself had proposed talking about her relationship with Olga in person, which meant that they'd discuss it when they met. He called her house—he didn't have her work number—and left a message, inviting her to dinner. If she was around, they could meet at their usual place, whenever was best for her. He'd be home around seven, waiting for her to confirm.

≋

Though Espinosa had asked the doorman to tell her that he was waiting for her, Irene wouldn't come downstairs until she heard his voice on the intercom. On the way to the car, parked only a few feet away, she kept glancing over her shoulder.

"Calm down. That's what they want, for you to get scared."

"Fuck, Espinosa, what do you expect? For me to act like nothing's happening? I'm not a cop. I'm not used to stuff like this."

They walked to the car arm in arm.

"Sorry, I'm just nervous."

"Fine. Don't worry. No one will dare try anything on you while we're together. Should we go back to our restaurant?"

As soon as they found a table, Espinosa asked Irene to tell him one more time what had happened.

"There's nothing besides what I already told you on the phone. On the corner of my block, there's a traffic light at the intersection with a much busier street. So the light is almost always red when you're driving on my street. It takes a long time to change. I have to take the cross street to get home, but I'm used to it, and since it's so close to my building I never worry about having to wait, because I'm practically home. When I came back from work tonight I stopped, as always, and waited for the light to change. Suddenly someone came up—I couldn't see who—and pressed a big For Sale sign against the passenger window, completely blocking my side view, and simultaneously trying to open the door. I got scared and hit the gas. The person kept trying to force the door with one of their hands while the other was pressing the board against the window. I managed to get away before the light changed; I didn't even worry if any cars were coming toward me."

"And you couldn't see who was behind the cardboard?"

"No. I don't know if I wanted to. I looked quickly in the rearview mirror, afraid they'd shoot me, but I couldn't see them. I was terrified. Espinosa, it's not a coincidence. I know that people hold up cars at stoplights, but that's a busy intersection, it was seven at night, there were other cars behind and on either side of mine, and the person was interested in me and only me. It's not a coincidence. Olga dies, then the fortune-teller dies, now they try to force open my car door a block from my house. . . . It wasn't a coincidence, and it wasn't some juvenile delinquent. I was struck by how they hid behind that sign. I know you don't agree, Espinosa, but this has something to do with that guy."

"There's no reason for him to try to kill you."

"He might be crazy, Espinosa."

"If he was crazy and wanted to kill you, he wouldn't

take so much trouble to avoid being identified; he'd just kill you."

"Who else can it be? I've never been threatened, I don't have any enemies, nobody's after me. All these things started after that fucking freak showed up."

"What things?"

"These deaths! Fuck, what else? Are you waiting for me to die too?"

"Try to calm down. Let's order some beers. If you want, you can stay with me this weekend. I'll take you to work and come get you at the end of the day."

"You can't do that for the rest of your life."

"That's another subject."

"Espinosa, don't play with me."

"I'm not playing. Besides, Gabriel's birthday is Saturday. Four days from now."

"And what does that have to do with anything?"

"Don't forget that his birthday is the expiration date for the fortune-teller's prediction."

"Jesus, Espinosa, are you crazy too?"

"No, but I'm used to taking other people's craziness into account."

They didn't speak about Olga; they were worn out. The night wasn't right for romance either; at least, that's how Espinosa interpreted Irene's turning down his invitation to spend the night. He escorted her home and she promised to be extra careful. She'd wait for him in the morning to take her to work. Espinosa accompanied her upstairs and said good-bye only after looking over her whole apartment—at her request.

Downstairs, he showed his badge to the doorman and made a series of recommendations about security. Then he left, satisfied that Irene was set for the night. Before he started his car's engine, he carefully scoured the street for anything suspicious; then he drove around the block, passing the building once again before heading toward the Peixoto District.

He was convinced that the episode hadn't been a simple attempted mugging. If you want to steal watches, jewelry, or a purse, you'd use the driver's window, almost always showing a weapon or hinting at its existence; you don't force the other door and hide behind a piece of cardboard. This person had tried to get into the car. And they probably didn't know how to drive, which would explain why they went for the passenger door.

The next morning, after picking up Irene and taking her to work, Espinosa went to the office. He wanted to think quietly about the "Gabriel case" before he completely lost track of it.

In his office, he gave orders to his assistants not to interrupt him unless it was absolutely necessary. He took a sheet of paper and wrote down all the names of everyone involved in the story, drew a circle around each one, and traced each person's link to everyone else involved. It wasn't that he believed this would be the solution to his problems; he was merely trying to keep things as uncomplicated as possible. The result expressed what was already obvious. Gabriel was the name that held all of them together. That had been expected, since the whole story had begun with him. Yet just because his name was at the hub didn't make him responsible for the deaths. Espinosa couldn't picture him threatening Irene at a stoplight in Ipanema. Why would he do something like that? Just to scare her? To kill her? He didn't need all those props. Unless Irene had invented the story of the attack to distract his attention from something else—like, for instance, her trip the weekend before.

He put aside the useless drawing, leaned back in his chair, crossed his hands behind his head, and let his mind run loose. The first figure to appear was Dona Alzira at the door of his building the day before. He put his chair back in its normal position, opened a drawer, and removed the bag she'd given him with the weapon and ammunition.

He unwrapped the revolver and held it in his hand for a while, trying to answer the question of what, exactly, Gabriel had been planning to do with a weapon. He pictured him firing at Hidalgo point-blank. It didn't work, though the idea wasn't completely absurd. In his desperate state of mind, it might have made sense. He put the revolver on top of the table and considered the box of bullets. It was clearly new. He arranged the bullets in the position they must have originally been packed in. They were loose. He stuck his finger in the leftover space and noticed that there would have been room for at least one more.

From his own box of bullets, he removed two .38 bullets and inserted them in the empty space. They fit perfectly. He separated his own bullets out and dumped the contents of the box on his desk. He counted them twice, then compared his calculation with the number printed on the box. Two were missing. Freire had surely used this box in the firing range, for the ballistics exam. But why two bullets? One would have been enough. He called the Criminology Institute. Freire wasn't in. He left a message for him to call as soon as possible. He sat wondering what had happened to the other bullet, assuming it hadn't been used in the tests, and couldn't imagine where else it might have ended up except in Hidalgo's head. After half an hour, Freire called. He'd removed only one bullet from the box, and nobody else had had access to it. Espinosa's head ached slightly; soon, he thought, it would ache more. He swallowed an aspirin, called in Welber, and told him what he was thinking.

"Espinosa, at first I thought the kid was guilty of everything, including his own craziness. But gradually my opinion changed, and I decided he was only a little crazy, but not responsible for the girl's death. Until he disappeared in the subway station and I found out later that the Chilean guy had been shot in the face only a few blocks away. If he wanted to kill the guy, why had he walked toward the subway station, which wasn't in the direction of the Chilean's house? Why didn't he go straight to the guy's building? If it was because he knew he was being followed, it seems unlikely that he would have gotten rid of me and then killed the guy. That would be tantamount to confessing to the crime. I'm sure he didn't kill the Chilean. Unless he's an extremely cold, calculating murderer who likes playing with his luck for the thrill of it all. But he doesn't seem like that kind of guy, though we've often been thrown off by innocent-looking people."

"I agree with you. And that's why I still haven't gone after him. And the ballistics results agree with me. But that missing bullet made me think of other possibilities."

"Like . . ."

"Like the following. He didn't shoot anybody—at least not in the last few years—with the gun the mother gave me, which she claimed was the one he always carried. But he could have used another weapon. Why would it have to be that one? Just because his mother says so? What if the mother, to protect the son, gave me a gun she knows hasn't been used?"

"Do you think she'd do that?"

"Welber, a mother will do anything to protect her son. Her husband taught her to use the weapon. She herself took the bullets out of the barrel and put them back in the box. She knows the difference between a revolver and a pistol. She knows that the caliber of her husband's gun was the same as the bullets her son had hidden away. She didn't hesitate to try to protect him."

"Does that mean he killed the girl too?"

"In my opinion, the same person killed them both. Think about it. Only someone Olga knew could get close enough to walk up to her on the platform and push her. And only a person who could be recognized would bother to hide their identity when they tried something against Irene."

"So you mean the guy suddenly goes from being completely innocent to completely guilty?"

"I'm not saying that he's guilty. I'm just saying it's not impossible.

"There's one thing," Espinosa went on, "about the guy that's intrigued me since our first meeting: the motive he claimed for meeting us, that he was worried about becoming a murderer. There could be a lot of fantasy in that story, but one thing seemed real enough: the fear that had overtaken him. He might even have been wrong about the nature of the threat, but he wasn't wrong about the intensity. What we still don't know—and what he still doesn't know—is what the threat really is."

"What about the Chilean?"

"The Chilean only sparked the crisis; he didn't cause it."

"Gabriel thinks that you don't consider him a suspect. And he was right, until an hour ago. Why don't we call him in for a more serious conversation?"

"I'd already decided to do that. Call and tell him I want to see him during his lunch hour. If he asks why, tell him it's to pick up his father's gun and clear up a few details."

"He's not going to be suspicious?"

"I don't think so. He's been here in the past and always came of his own free will."

"And what if he has some excuse to avoid coming today?"

"Tell him it's important, that the conversation can't be

put off. Don't pressure him with anything official; that might scare him off. He still feels like someone's after him. Tell him that between one and two will be fine. And, Welber . . ."

"Yes?"

"I'd like you to be there too."

⌐

The meeting didn't take place in Espinosa's office, but in the small conference room. When he entered, followed by Espinosa and Welber, Gabriel immediately noticed that not only the setting had changed. The weapon and the box of bullets were on the table.

"What happened?" His tone of voice and facial expression were different than they had been at previous encounters.

"That's what we'd like to know."

"How do you mean?"

"We know that you've committed the idiocy of walking around with a gun for the last few days."

"Who said that?"

"No use denying it. It doesn't make any difference."

"I was scared."

"Which is why you asked me for help. But that wasn't a good enough reason to walk around with a gun, ready to shoot the first suspicious-looking person you came across."

"I wasn't going to shoot anyone."

"Somebody who walks down the street with a loaded

thirty-eight has a hard time convincing me he didn't plan to shoot anyone."

"It was only for self-defense."

"Shooting people in self-defense."

"Everyone has the right to defend themselves."

"Not by carrying a gun. That's a crime punishable by imprisonment, with no parole."

"I didn't shoot anyone."

"Is that the weapon you were carrying?"

"That's my father's revolver."

"We know that. We want to know if this is the revolver you've been carrying."

"It is."

"And is this the ammunition with which you loaded the weapon?"

"It is . . . but I didn't shoot anyone."

"Did you buy it yourself?"

"That's right."

"Where?"

"In a store downtown."

"Nobody else knew about this box of bullets?"

"No."

"Then would you like to tell me where the missing bullet is?"

"What?"

"The bullet. One bullet is missing from the box. What happened to it?"

"I don't know. I didn't know one was missing."

"Would it have been used, perhaps?"

"Used, how?"

"The way thirty-eight-caliber bullets are usually used. To kill someone."

"Kill?"

"Yes, kill. The Chilean, for instance."

"Are you accusing me of—"

"No. I'm only giving an example and asking for an answer to my question. What happened to the missing bullet?"

"I don't know. I didn't know one was missing. Maybe it was missing to begin with. Maybe I dropped it on the floor."

"Maybe it was used on someone. . . ."

Over the next two hours, Espinosa and Welber went over the same questions, and Gabriel repeatedly had to walk them through his activities on the night of the Chilean's death, from the moment he left work until he got home. How he carried the gun, in his belt or pocket; whether he took out the bullets every time he got home, or if he always kept the revolver loaded; if he told his mother he was carrying a gun; how he managed to hide it from his colleagues. Espinosa finally wrapped up the discussion.

"I'd like you to come back tomorrow so we can take your deposition. Today was just a conversation."

Farewells were said without any friendliness.

"What did you think?" Welber wanted to know.

"I think something's not quite right. Every time we

repeated a question, he responded to it the exact same way—same details, almost the same words. It seemed a little rehearsed. When you tell a story several times, your natural tendency is to change a detail, add another one, fill in a gap, not just repeat the same thing verbatim. Even if he's not guilty, he's hiding something."

At the end of the afternoon, Espinosa picked up Irene, as planned, and they headed to the Peixoto District together. Espinosa had bought bread, food, and wine, planning an intimate meal for the cold weather, which had gotten worse over the last couple of days.

"You really think I need to stay at your place?"

"I'd like you to."

"But it's not necessary?"

"If not necessary, at least preferable. I don't have any way to put you under police protection. Officially, there's no case or registered complaint; we don't even have an investigation opened. I feel better with you here with me. I sent two detectives to tail Gabriel until the end of the weekend. After that, we'll see."

"How long do you think this is going to go on?"

"I think the end is near."

"You sound like a preacher."

They stayed home. They enjoyed the food and wine. It was nice, with the music. They went to bed, lulled by the sound of the wind that was blowing outside the windows.

He didn't ask, but Irene talked about her relationship with Olga. She confirmed what Espinosa had suspected: they had been lovers when they lived in São Paulo.

The night was different. Not better or worse than the previous nights. Different.

9

The following day, at the hour he had scheduled to speak with Gabriel, Dona Alzira climbed the stairs and paused for a minute in the small hallway that led to Espinosa's office. She checked her clothes (dark and sober, as the moment required) and smoothed her hair. She stood, as if at a bus stop, until a man came out whom she recognized as a policeman.

"May I help you, ma'am?"

"I'd like to speak with Officer Espinosa."

"What is it regarding?"

"I've come to testify."

"Were you asked to testify?"

"Of course not."

"Then can you tell me what it's regarding? The officer is in a meeting."

"Just tell him it's Gabriel's mother."

After glancing at a chair the detective offered her, Dona Alzira thanked him and remained on her feet. A few minutes later, the door to Espinosa's office opened and two men emerged, one of whom she recognized. Officer Espinosa followed.

"Dona Alzira, to what do I owe this visit?"

"It's not a visit. I came to testify instead of my son."

"Ma'am, you can't do that. He was required to appear, not you."

"I know that, Officer, but my testimony can clear up the facts involving my son's name."

"Dona Alzira, we appreciate your help, but right now we're interested in talking to your son, not to you."

"But you will be, Officer. Gabriel had nothing to do with those deaths; he was only the recipient of those people's evil."

"Dona Alzira, it's the job of the police to decide if he's implicated or not."

"You're right about that, Officer, but I think you'll change your mind once you hear what I have to say."

"In order to give a deposition, you need to be accompanied by a lawyer."

"The presence of a lawyer won't make any difference to what I have to say."

"I'm willing to listen to you, Dona Alzira, but I want to make clear that what you have to say doesn't mean that Gabriel doesn't have to come in as well."

Welber was called, the door was closed, and the people sitting outside Espinosa's office were informed that he was not to be interrupted.

"What facts are you referring to, ma'am, when you say your son has nothing to do with them?"

"I'm referring to the deaths of the girl and the foreigner."

"Why do you say that your son has nothing to do with them?"

"It's not that he has nothing to do with them; in fact, he was the starting point for the events—or, rather, not so much him, but the foreigner's prediction. He was only the victim."

"There are strong links between your son and those deaths."

"My son didn't kill those people."

"Why do you say that, ma'am?"

"Because I did."

Espinosa and Welber leaned toward Dona Alzira, as if to hear something they hadn't quite caught.

"What are you saying, Dona Alzira?"

"Just what you heard. I killed them."

Her voice was steady and unafraid. There was no anger in it: there was haughtiness and pride, as if awaiting praise for the crimes she had just confessed. Dona Alzira didn't even move her hands, crossed on top of the purse she was hugging to her body.

"Ma'am, are you aware of the implications of what you've just said?"

"Of course I am. I'm confessing to two murders, even though I don't consider them to be murders."

"Did you act in self-defense?"

"In a manner of speaking. Not in my own defense, but in my son's."

"And can you tell me how you killed them?"

"Of course. But it will take a while."

"Don't worry about that; we've got all the time you need."

"Well, it's hard to say exactly when it all started. I might say it was when Father Crisóstomo refused to help me combat evil. I think he's old, he's lost the strength of the old Christian soldiers, he's gotten too comfortable. He was a tiger when he still believed in exorcism, but now he's a house cat. I told him that my Gabriel had been taken over by the forces of evil, that we had to do something quickly before he was destroyed, but Father Crisóstomo didn't pay me any mind. He said that all Gabriel needed was to get married and start a family—as if he didn't have a family already, as if I didn't exist, as if there was some void that another woman needed to fill. Men don't understand what it is for someone to come out of your own body, to be part of you, and to still be part of your body even after they leave it. You'll never know what it is to be a mother."

"I don't see what this has to do with the deaths."

"Everything, Officer. When something attacks my son, it attacks my own body; when something attacks his soul, it attacks my soul as well. So as soon as I heard about the prediction that spirit of darkness had made, I didn't have any doubt that he was an agent of evil. And my son also understood that, which is why he came to you to ask for protection and help. And you were a good man, Officer. But evil is insidious; it takes over every inch of even the best man; it subverts him, and that's what happened to you. Evil takes on unpredictable forms, and the most powerful of them all comes in the form of woman. You didn't realize it, but just after the foreigner's prophecy, the demon appeared in the form of two women. One for Gabriel, one for you, trying to break down your souls. So much that you, sir, who had listened to my son's problem with sympathy, were soon in love with one of them, completely taken over by her. The same thing happened with Gabriel, but he resisted more. Didn't you notice how much the two looked alike? In fact, they were two forms of the same being. I managed to destroy one of them."

Espinosa was speechless. Welber, as he was taking all of this down, looked at the woman in front of him, who was confessing to two murders as if she'd stolen her neighbor's pudding recipe.

"Can you give us the details of how you carried out these two murders?"

"That's what I'm doing. The girl took more work. I started riding the subway with her. Gabriel had told me that sometimes they met in the subway on the way to work, and he'd mentioned the name of her station. I started taking the same train. I never introduced myself. I let her get used to seeing me on the platform. I needed a few days before the ideal conditions appeared. One day, when the train was approaching and the crowd was moving toward it, I saw her at the edge of the platform. It was perfect, better than I'd ever expected. As soon as the train entered the station, I pretended to trip, and with a little nudge of the shoulder everything was taken care of. Nobody noticed what had happened before she fell on the tracks, and even if they had the most they could have said is that they saw a lady lose her balance and bump into the girl. A tragic accident. But nobody noticed anything. I took advantage of the confusion, left the station, and got in a cab."

Dona Alzira looked at Espinosa as if expecting a compliment. Welber took down the last sentences and Espinosa waited for the next part of the story. After a few seconds, the noise of computer keys was replaced by the continuous sound of traffic coming through the closed window.

"And what about the foreigner?"

"That was easier, since I didn't need to prepare. Gabriel had gotten his address in a hospital, and wanted to meet with him to clear everything up. But my son is pure, Officer. He doesn't know what evil is; he doesn't know the schemes of Satan. I decided to act before he could, especially when I realized that he'd bought a gun. One morning, before he woke up, I switched the gun he carried in his coat pocket for my husband's old revolver. They were the same weight and size; he wouldn't notice the difference. As soon as he left for work, I went to the guy's address. It was a ground-floor apartment. I rang the bell, but nobody was home. I came back in the afternoon, but there was still nobody there. The building doesn't have a doorman or anyone to watch over the garage, because there isn't a garage. I went back one more time in the evening and stood waiting in a small alleyway outside the building. After more than an hour I saw the couple arrive, and then I saw the light come on inside the apartment. I decided to ring the doorbell and fire as soon as the door was opened, and I was already walking toward the door when I heard the sound of the side window being opened. The window was protected by burglar bars and was only a few inches above my head. When the man finished raising the blinds and the window, I moved close and whispered his name. He came up to the window to see who was calling him. I lifted the revolver and fired. To my surprise, nobody showed up after the shot. It was during prime time, so everyone else in the building was watching TV. I heard the woman scream. I put the gun in my purse and left in the dark, toward the street. There was nobody around. I kept walking casually down the sidewalk, and after a block I came upon the São João Batista cemetery. I walked toward the chapel and saw that they were holding services on the second floor. I thought I'd be safe there. As soon as I entered, I went to the toilet; I needed to get rid of the gun and I didn't want to throw it onto the street—I didn't know if it was registered. In the bathroom I removed the bullets and stuck them in my purse with the gun. I saw a room where there were only two women talking, standing in the doorway. I waited for them to leave. Inside, there was only a coffin with a dead man. I went in, made the sign of the cross, and stuck the gun under the body. It was all very quick; nobody saw me enter or leave."

At that point, Dona Alzira paused.

"Backing up a little," said Espinosa, "when you were in the alleyway waiting for the fortune-teller—was there any light there?"

"No. I don't think so. If there was any light, it was really weak. It was dark."

"Were there any garbage cans? According to your account, it's a service area."

"I don't remember. As I said, it was dark; I couldn't see what might be there in the alleyway."

"But you'd been there during the day. You don't remember any details about it?"

"I was focused on the movement in the building. I don't remember details like that. I was worried about the fortune-teller."

"When you left the cemetery chapel, what did you do?"

"I just walked out, as if I was leaving a wake, which in fact I was. I got on a bus. I arrived home right before Gabriel did and put the bullets in the box, which I knew he'd hidden away. When he walked in, we talked about whether he should leave his revolver with me. I don't even think he noticed that the guns had been switched."

"Why did you take the trouble to bring the other gun to me?"

"Because I knew you'd have it examined. Since it wasn't the crime weapon, any suspicion that Gabriel had done it would be removed. I didn't think that you'd count the bullets and notice that one was missing. When Gabriel told me last night that you'd interrogated him about that, I decided that it was time to clear everything up. And that's what I'm doing now."

"Are you aware that you're confessing to two murders?"

"Officer, I'm completely aware of everything I'm doing."

"Does anyone else know about this?"

"My father confessor."

"And Gabriel?"

"My son doesn't know anything. I'd rather you didn't tell him; I need to do that myself."

There followed a long silence, which Espinosa interpreted as a sign that the confession was over.

"Detective Welber will print out a copy of your deposition. After reading it carefully, I'd like you to sign it."

"Are you going to arrest me?"

"No. You came here of your own free will, and we know your address, so there's no need to arrest you. Besides, we need to confirm several parts of your story. Do you remember which room it was in the chapel where you hid the gun?"

"It was on the second floor. In two of the rooms there were a lot of people; the others were empty. It won't be hard to find."

"I'd like you to come back tomorrow, along with your son and a lawyer."

"Why my son? What do you still want to know?"

"I told you that your testifying doesn't mean that he doesn't have to. Besides, there are still some details—"

"Why don't you ask now?"

"Because it's important that your son be there."

Welber handed Espinosa her testimony, and he passed it to Dona Alzira.

"Please, see if this reflects what you've told us."

Dona Alzira read the deposition carefully, signed it, and handed it back to Espinosa. Then she got up, fixed her hair, said good-bye without offering her hand, and walked toward the door, grasping her purse to her chest with both hands.

≋

"Espinosa, that lady could take out an army."

"I agree. You can do that by pressing a button. There's a big difference between that and firing in a man's face from a few inches away, or pushing a girl under the wheels of a train."

"Do you think she's lying?"

"Just because she's confessed doesn't mean it's true. The story about hiding the gun in the coffin is obviously true—she couldn't make that up. But whether she did it herself is another story. We'll have to exhume the body. Try to find out whom the two ladies were mourning on the second floor of the chapel."

≋

On Friday morning, Espinosa ate breakfast alone again. Irene had gone back home the day before. The walk to the station took place under a gray and windy sky. The day passed without either Dona Alzira or Gabriel putting in an appearance. Espinosa sent them a written subpoena. No word from Irene. He didn't call either. That night, he fell asleep reading a crime novel he thought he might have already read. He drifted off to the sound of trees shaken by the wind. The next day was Saturday.

~

When, the next morning, he opened his door to get the newspaper, he was greeted by Petita, who was frenetically wagging her tail while waiting for her owner to make it up the last flight of stairs.

"I brought your paper from downstairs."

"Thanks, Alice. We still aren't seeing very much of each other, are we?"

"You seem to be busy."

Espinosa thought she was being ironic, but he pretended not to notice. Alice knew that he wasn't very talkative before breakfast.

"Next week you can pick up Neighbor. Don't you want to visit him one more time before he comes over?"

"Fine. Tomorrow morning we'll visit our friend."

The coffeemaker was plugged in and the bread was in the toaster. Espinosa glanced at the headlines, took his first sip of coffee, and the telephone rang. It was Irene, suggesting lunch. At least she wasn't in São Paulo. The toast popped up, he took another sip of coffee, and the phone rang again. He thought it must be Irene again, adding something to the message. He got up to answer.

"Officer Espinosa?"

"Yes."

"My mother died."

"Gabriel! Where are you?"

"At home . . . with her."

"How did she die?"

"Gas."

"How do you know she's dead?"

"There's no doubt."

"Did you tell anybody?"

"No."

"I'm on my way."

He gulped down the rest of the coffee, called Welber, rattled off some instructions, got dressed, and left. When he reached the building in Flamengo, Gabriel opened the door before he could even ring the bell. He was barefoot, wearing shorts and a sweater with no shirt beneath it. His hair was rumpled.

"I opened the windows and shut off the gas. I didn't touch the body. I couldn't."

Espinosa could still smell the gas. Ground-floor apartments are hard to air out, and Gabriel hadn't opened the living-room door. Dona Alzira was seated on the floor in front of the oven; the door was open. Espinosa figured she'd been dead for several hours, probably since the early morning.

"She closed the kitchen door and the window, covered the cracks with tape, and turned on all the burners on the range and the oven. I only found her this morning, when I woke up. She was careful to cover the crack under my bedroom door with a wet towel, from the other side."

"Did she leave a note?"

"No."

"Were you with her last night?"

"We had dinner together. We went to bed early."

"What did you talk about over dinner?"

"Nothing special. We didn't talk much."

"Did she tell you about her deposition the day before yesterday?"

"What deposition? She gave a deposition Thursday?"

"I'll talk to you about it later. She didn't say anything at dinner that hinted at what she was going to do?"

"She was a little anxious and said she was going to take a sleeping pill. It was a normal conversation."

Espinosa called the Ninth Precinct, three blocks away, and told them what had happened. Fifteen minutes later, two policemen arrived. Espinosa explained that he'd been called first because he knew the family. He let the detectives conduct the preliminary investigations. The forensic people arrived a few minutes later. Espinosa stayed in the apartment for a while, waiting for Gabriel to change clothes and answer the detectives' questions. He left the numbers where he could be reached.

On his way home, Espinosa thought about how odd it was for an almost sixty-year-old lady, profoundly religious and until then morally irreproachable, to seek out a policeman to confess, not without pride, that she'd coldly and with premeditation murdered two people she didn't even know on the basis that they were servants of the devil. She believed she'd acted in legitimate defense of her son, and she didn't feel the least bit of guilt for what she'd done. The day after her confession, she had dinner with her son, said good night, and killed herself without so much as leaving a note. Espinosa wasn't sure the story hung together very well.

Once he got back home, he made himself another cup of coffee. The wind was still blowing in the square outside. He called Welber again. He asked him to make copies of Dona Alzira's deposition and send them to the Ninth, Tenth, and Nineteenth Precincts, together with the report on her suicide. He would call again later to explain.

That afternoon, he picked up Irene. They chose a restaurant on the Avenida Atlântica, facing the sea, even though he wasn't convinced that the ocean view would erase the image of Dona Alzira on the kitchen floor.

"What aren't you telling me?"

"Gabriel's mother."

"What about her?"

"She died."

"She died?"

"Killed herself."

"Because of her son?"

"It seems it was because of herself."

Espinosa explained about the confession and repeated what Gabriel had said about his mother's suicide.

"Espinosa, I don't think that woman committed those crimes."

"Did you know her?"

"I've never seen her in my life, but I don't think that a sixty-year-old lady would commit two murders in such cold blood."

"She was a religious fanatic. Precisely because they're religious fanatics, certain people feel the need to go around killing the agents of evil."

"And what happens now?"

"Now she's dead, and copies of her testimony are being sent to the three precincts involved."

"Do the confession and suicide mean that the case is closed?"

"For the other precincts, probably."

"And for you?"

"Not quite. The gun hidden in the coffin will confirm Dona Alzira's story—she wouldn't make that up, knowing we could check it—and the other precincts will be happy to chalk up one more case solved. But in fact nothing is clear. Not even her suicide."

"She didn't kill herself?"

"I can't swear it. Technically, Gabriel could have killed his mother. The sleeping pill he said she took could have been tampered with. She was small and thin; it wouldn't have been hard to move the body from her bedroom to the kitchen, and then all he'd have to do was turn on the gas."

"But what about the details in her deposition? She couldn't have made it all up."

"She could have heard it from her son."

"You're just speaking hypothetically, though, aren't you?"

"Of course. She could very well have committed suicide. We've lost the possibility of cross-examining her in front

of her son. With her death, the deposition seems rein-
forced, which is very convenient for Gabriel."

"What do you think really happened?"

"What I think is pretty far-fetched for a police investigation."

Espinosa stared out at the sea for a few seconds, seem-
ingly captured by the beauty of the scene, and then looked
back at Irene.

"Let's do a little exercise. There's no proof, or even any
hint, that backs up what I'm saying—it's only speculation.
When Gabriel came to see me the first time, he was hon-
estly feeling threatened by the Chilean's prediction. He
wasn't playing with me or acting in bad faith—he gen-
uinely believed he would kill someone before his next
birthday. We were the ones who couldn't understand that
as truth. Instead of focusing on Gabriel, we zeroed in on
the Chilean, about how he was a fraud, a charlatan, all that;
but the real question wasn't whether he was telling the
truth. It was whether Gabriel was telling the truth. The
only reason for someone to be so terrified about a barroom
fortune-teller's prophecy is if it was on the mark. But
Gabriel himself thought the idea of his killing someone
was absurd. How could we make that absurdity make
sense? The answer, I think, is that Gabriel was feeling
guilty for a murder he'd already committed. What the
fortune-teller said was true; he just got the time frame
wrong: future instead of past. Gabriel had directly or indirectly caused the death of someone, long ago. What the

Chilean did was reactivate that crime. That's why Gabriel's terror was legitimate."

"But . . . who did Gabriel kill?"

"His father."

"His father?"

"Right."

"Jesus, Espinosa, I know you said that you let your imagination run wild. Can you tell me how he killed his father?"

"Closing the door."

"What?"

"Closing the bathroom door."

"I don't get it."

"As I said, it's just an imaginary exercise. It might have happened something like this: it was winter, and the house they lived in was old and didn't have a separate shower; it just had a bathtub with a hand-held nozzle and a gas water heater. A plastic curtain around the tub completed the scene. Dona Alzira's husband liked to take full baths, a habit he'd probably acquired in the hotels he frequented with less religious women. Dona Alzira turned on the hot water, prepared his bath, and closed the window. Maybe on a similar occasion Gabriel had heard his mother's critical comments about his father's bath habit. Then one of two things could have happened. First, Dona Alzira could have said that she was going to the supermarket while her husband was in the bath. On her way out, she could have asked her son to close the bathroom door so that he wouldn't get cold. What she didn't say was that the heater was as old as the house, and that the exhaust pipe was blocked. Or, second possibility, the mother leaves without saying anything and Gabriel simply closes the bathroom door to avoid seeing his father, because he associates the bathtub with the times his father's cheated on his mother. In both versions, death by carbon monoxide poisoning is almost certain. That happened a few days before Gabriel's tenth birthday."

"You really are nuts."

"No more than most people."

"And who killed Olga and the Chilean?"

"Probably Gabriel, but I don't dismiss the possibility of the mother having killed Olga; she was resentful, and she viewed women as a form of evil."

"And what about what happened to me?"

"Probably just a smoke screen—too much of a pantomime to be relevant."

"Is all this what you really think happened, or is it just a fantasy?"

"Some of the details might not be exactly right, but I think that's more or less it. Now it doesn't matter; there's no way to prove it. Dona Alzira's testimony and death put an end to the story. If we find the gun under the dead guy, that will simply confirm what she said. Even if the autopsy reveals an abnormal dosage of sleeping pills in her bloodstream, it won't be considered suspicious—it seems normal that a suicide would want to suffer as little as possible when she turns on the gas. So I think that's the end of the story. One thing, though, is sure: if I'm right, the Chilean's prediction came true. Today is Gabriel's birthday."

"What's going to happen to him?"

"For now, nothing. After a while, I think he'll get in touch with me. I can't imagine him all by himself in that gray, dark apartment, living with the truth behind those deaths, without going crazy. I don't know what will come first: the confession or the madness."

Even though it was Saturday afternoon, the beach was deserted and there were few people walking on the sidewalk that ran along the sand. A wide window ran across the front of the restaurant, shielding them from the powerful southwesterly wind, which had been blowing for two days now. The greenish-gray sea and sky contrasted with the white foam thrown up by the wind; the ragged clouds let flashes of sunlight glance off the water.